SPELLS AND SANDWICHES

KATE MOSEMAN

FORTUNELLA PRESS

Previously published as *Undercover Paranormal*.

Cover by ArcaneCovers.com

ISBN 978-1-957320-02-1 (ebook)

ISBN 978-1-957320-22-9 (paperback)

Fortunella Press

For my little black poodle,
who can't read this,
but would very much enjoy chewing it

It was a good day to arrive in New York City.
No one expected me. Everything awaited me.

—Patti Smith, *Just Kids*

I was supposed to be finding a place to stay, not playing dress-up as Snow White at a children's party. The hem of the sparkly dress only came to mid-calf—they hadn't had time to lengthen it to match my height—but that just made it easier to hoist the layered skirts and run up the immaculate steps of the white limestone townhouse.

I pounded on the door.

Solid wood. Faceted glass windows. Fancy. You had to have serious money for a place like this on the Upper East Side. Only a few blocks but a world away from the tiny apartment where I used to visit my grandma for the summer. "Entertainment's here," I called.

The door opened a crack, revealing a face that went from neutral to disapproving in half a second.

"Zelda Hawkins, at your service." I swept a bow, then straightened the crown, which was currently trying to rip a flesh wound in my scalp, and gave the beady eye in the doorway a rakish smile before trying again. "Snow White? For the party?"

One eyebrow rose.

"I'm with Lily." My cousin Luella's daughter. Nice kid. Fashion major at NYU. Made money on the side by dressing up herself and her friends as fairytale characters and showing up at rich people's parties. When she asked me to fill in for a sick Snow White, I couldn't say no. Lily was family, even if we'd hardly ever seen each other.

The door swung open like it might snap shut if I didn't dive through, so I didn't hesitate. Inside, I met the full gaze of a housekeeper who appeared to already have second thoughts about letting in the riff-raff. "Down the hall, on the right," she said.

"Thanks." I threw her a salute and meant it. I knew what it was like to work long hours for not enough money. She seemed to smile in spite of herself as I bolted past, my sturdy boots making a light squeak on the marble floor.

Wide doors were thrown open to reveal a parlor lit by the afternoon sun. Cream-colored furniture with tasteful touches of gold filled the room. The footrests had skirts, and a sparkling crystal chandelier hung above. Everything was pristine—and probably wildly expensive.

It was an excellent setting for royalty, even if the current crop was a bunch of college students in costumes. And there was Lily, in a purple satin Rapunzel dress. She looked like a younger version of her mother, Luella—only instead of having blonde hair mixed with gray, like my cousin, Lily was still as blonde as whipped honey.

Nearby, Cinderella and Prince Charming mingled with a horde of small children in new-looking clothing.

I shuddered. Small children. Not my forte. But you do what you have to do.

Lily caught sight of me and beamed. She clapped her hands in storybook delight. "Look, Snow White is here!"

I took a deep breath and stepped into the room. One boot slid behind the other in an improvised curtsy. I sank into it, happy that my joints were all managing to cooperate. I could do this.

The noise in the room hushed.

I looked up.

"Your shoes are all wrong," observed one of the little monsters in pigtails.

Who did this kid think she was, the junior fashion police? I straightened and stuck my right foot out. "Didn't you know? Snow White always wears Doc Martens."

The kid's skeptical look could have been sold by the pound.

"She's too old to be Snow White, anyway," added another little monster.

Seriously? Knocking my shoes was one thing—but my age? Snow White nearly let out a few choice un-children's-party-appropriate words. But this was family on the line, so Snow White kept her mouth shut and instead glared several vanadium steel knives in the monsters' direction.

Lily stepped delicately through the crowd and gave me a quick hug. Her hair was pulled back and somehow attached to an extra-long Rapunzel braid. "You look great, Zelda." Her gaze slipped to my Doc Martens, briefly, before darting upward again.

"Thank you. Sorry I didn't fit into any of the slippers. Size ten-and-a-half princess shoes are tough to find."

"I like your boots. Snow White would have done better in boots."

A bell-like tone rang through the room.

I snorted. "They have an actual *gong*?"

Turning toward the sound revealed a second set of doors opening to the next room. Through the doorway, a table held four triple-decker naked cakes, the kind where you can see the frosting layers. Two vanilla funfetti cakes, and two dark chocolate cakes piled with white vanilla icing.

Chocolate and vanilla: The bases were covered. My mouth watered involuntarily. It'd been a long time since the expired granola bar I'd dry-swallowed for breakfast.

A woman stepped into the doorway. She was dressed in that quiet style that manages to look both plain and incredibly wealthy at the same time. Too well-preserved to be called young. Too unlined to be called old. Same as any carefully pressed woman you might see alighting from a tinted-window SUV in the Upper East Side—except for one thing.

Her hair. White as restaurant china, a perfect frame around her ageless face.

My fists clenched.

Why?

It was like I had a word on the tip of my tongue. And whatever word it was, it wasn't a pleasant one.

"Cake," she said, warm and modulated, almost husky. Cultured. Her lips formed the word crisply, without the need for volume.

"Cake!" the kids howled as one, rushing past her through the open doors.

"Cake," I echoed to myself. The word tasted wrong. It definitely wasn't the one my instincts were trying to shove into the front of my head. I unclenched my fists, slowly.

Lily released my arm to move into position for pictures, and I stood there like an idiot, a scruffy statue to go with the rest of the marble ones in the house.

Get a grip and smile, Snow White.

One foot went in front of the other until I had reached the cake, and Lily, and her friends.

That woman was standing off to the side.

Don't *stare*, for God's sake.

Smile.

The cameras flashed.

Smile, damn it.

My teeth were so exposed they dried, making my upper lip cling to the enamel in an unintentional snarl. The camera flash made me think of that moment in a horror movie where a strobe of light suddenly illuminates a herky-jerky monster scuttling through the shadows.

What was wrong with me?

Grandma might have known. I wished—not for the first time—that I still had her guidance. That I hadn't pushed away my magic after she died. That I'd been old enough to take over the family sandwich shop she'd proudly operated on the Upper West Side.

Wishful thoughts, all of them. But I was here, now. And once I took care of this little obligation, my new life would begin. The family restaurant would be restored if I had to work till I bled.

I licked my teeth and tried to rearrange my expression into something less deranged.

With picture time complete, the white-haired woman moved into position to cut the first cake. We storybook characters flanked her. She lifted a chef's kiss of a knife, patterned finish with some kind of hardwood handle, but what else would you expect in a setting so rich.

Whatever was giving me the heebie-jeebies would soon be in my rearview mirror. Figuratively, since I'd sold my car for cash before I arrived.

Then a scuffle erupted behind her.

Two boys grabbed at each other's Little Lord Fauntleroy jackets. They lost their balance and tripped, crashing into the woman from behind. Sunlight pinged off the Damascus steel as she flew forward with the knife extended. My heart had time for one big thud before screams flew up from all around.

With reflexes honed in restaurant kitchens and after-hours bars, I stepped inside her reach and seized her wrist, twisting upward to point the knife out of harm's way. We stumbled together, my larger size counterbalancing her smaller frame until we both stood upright again.

Up close, she smelled like powdery violets and iron.

And right then, I knew: I shouldn't have touched her.

I should have let her accidentally skewer someone, in that pristine white drawing room, and then I should have run all the way back to Florida, on foot if necessary.

But even as I let go, I knew it was too late.

My hand began to tingle.

"Damn it," I said, softly, not for the benefit of the little ears—they could handle a few swears—but because all the air had left my lungs.

I looked at my hand helplessly as red vines with sharp thorns spread across my palm like glitter-covered henna. Invisible, electrified pins and needles sank into my veins, swept to my shoulder, spread across my chest, and through the rest of my body. I pressed my lips together. No way I was going to cry out in front of Lily. Or these little party gremlins.

My grandmother's voice echoed: *Let the magic in.*

"Oh, Grandma," I murmured to myself, watching the red vines writhe on my skin, "what if I wanted to keep it out?"

When I looked up, the woman was watching me. Her irises glowed red like a dying broiler element. Like blood.

Of course. One of *them*. Yet no one else flinched. They couldn't see it. If they could, they would have been screaming, and not for ice cream.

I knew the Upper East Side was a hotspot for rich old vampires. I just didn't expect to run into one of them at a children's party.

Her red gaze was so mesmerizing it was hard to look away, but I managed to turn my head. The mirror across the room reflected my crown, which had slid sideways again, and the slightly smeared lipstick on my mouth—

Which now matched the red glow in my eyes. I winced, squeezed my eyes shut, then reopened them. Their red reflection still glowed in the mirror. "Double damn it." I'd let the magic in, all right. Whether I wanted to or not.

The white-haired woman's gaze followed mine to the mirror. "Are you quite well?" So mellow and elegant, but her eyes were nothing of the sort. And she still held the knife.

When had I seen those eyes before?

Now Lily was moving toward us. She hadn't shown any signs of magic yet, and her side of the family hadn't told her our family secret—ignorance, meet bliss—but just because she couldn't see any of it didn't mean she wasn't smart enough to pick up on something weird going on.

I instinctively put my hands behind my back. "I'm going upstairs for a second," I called to Lily, before she got any closer. "Wardrobe malfunction."

The woman smiled like a cat with feathers hanging off its lips. "This way, please." She took my arm. She was stronger than she looked. Powdery violets and iron, indeed.

I could have fought her off.

I think.

But I let her guide me to the stairs before shaking her hand loose.

"Go ahead," she said, gesturing to the stairs for me to go first.

I nodded to the knife she was still carrying. "Won't they need that to cut the cake?"

She placed it carefully on a marble-topped side table.

Better. "After you," I said.

2

I followed her to the second floor. The pins and needles sensation had almost faded, leaving behind a giddiness that made the twisting stairs feel like a carnival ride. Only faint tracings of the thorny red vines remained.

We entered a bedroom with crimson walls, polished hardwood floors, and drawn curtains. It still had touches of gold and crystal, but where the genteel parlor had invited in the sun, this one closed it out entirely.

The perfectly-made bed piled with heaps of pillows made me forget about vampires for one brief, shining second. This room called out for a set of freshly-washed PJs and a well-deserved midday nap.

Instead, I scanned the furniture for something small and heavy. There was a gold candlestick on the vanity that would work in a pinch. I scooped it up and tossed it from hand to hand.

She closed the door. "You don't remember me."

"Should I?"

She waited.

We both glanced, simultaneously, in the mirror above the vanity. Two pairs of red eyes reflected back at us. Her white hair looked pure next to my unruly mix of dark strands and gray streaks that swept from my temples and my crown.

Something about her *was* familiar. The red vine tracings, or the strange tingling sensation as the magic took hold, could have come from any vampire. But the character of it—the soul of it—

This wasn't the first time I'd felt it.

"I've mirrored your powers before, haven't I?"

She met my gaze. "A long time ago."

"The last time I did anything like that, I was a child." I paused, unfurling the timeline in my mind. "In Central Park. With my grandmother." This woman must have known Grandma from *way* back. "She used to—"

"Bring people to meet you."

"Yes."

"To teach you to copy their magic."

I couldn't help glancing at my hands. "Yes."

"So many times—so many people—that you do not even remember me."

Now there was a challenge if I ever heard one. I studied her face. No more clues there than I'd already seen. Then I gazed at her hands, and the memory glowed brighter. My grandmother's introduction: *Zelda, I want you to meet someone. This is Miss...*

I snapped my fingers. "Laguerre."

"Call me Victorine. Just because I am Blessed does not mean we must be formal with one another."

Blessed. You could hear the capital letter when she said it. I hadn't heard that term in a long time. They weren't called vampires, not out loud, not if you had any sense. You called them by their nickname—a quirk they had, an exception to the traditional vampire lore: their ability to enter sacred ground. It probably didn't make up for the fact that an old spell had trapped them in Manhattan, the better to keep them from causing havoc everywhere else.

Even if Victorine said she wanted to be on a first-name basis, I still needed to tread carefully. You couldn't trust them—although Grandma must have been friendly with this one for some reason.

Her gaze turned curious, like I was a stuffed specimen in the Museum of Natural History. "Your magic. Is it like your grandmother's? Does it also last a day or two?"

"You knew her well enough to know how her magic worked?"

"We were on the same side. I like to think we were friends."

"I haven't used my abilities in a long time."

"You jest."

"Magic was something I did with Grandma. When she died . . ." I looked away, cleared my throat. "Not that it's any of your business." I set the candlestick down with a *thunk*. "I'm beginning to think ending up here wasn't exactly an accident. What did you do? Send one of your Initiates to incapacitate the other Snow White?"

"I have no Initiates."

"You did the dirty work yourself, then."

"Why didn't your parents take over your grandmother's sandwich shop when she died?"

I blinked at the sudden change of subject. "My parents didn't want to run Grandma's sandwich shop. We lived in Florida." In fact, all of my grandmother's descendants were in Florida at that point, but were either too young or too rooted to be interested in taking over.

"Were you surprised to find the landlord kept the property vacant?"

"*Kept* it vacant?" When Lily moved to New York and found the location boarded up, we all assumed it had only been that way a short while.

She shook her head slightly, like you would when a small child doesn't understand something. "One last question: Have you ever wondered why the lease was offered to you at a price far below the going rate?"

Unease crawled through my belly and settled tightly around my lungs. "Um... rent control?"

She laughed. "Oh, no. The offer was extended to you to *bring you home*." She picked up the candlestick I'd abandoned and placed it in its original position, as precisely as a chess move. "I was your grandmother's landlord. And now I'm yours."

My grandmother's landlord?

And now mine?

It seemed like a power play. Like she thought she'd maneuvered me right where she wanted.

She didn't realize that recklessness ran in my family like a swirl of cayenne through cake frosting.

"I don't care if you're my landlord or the Queen of May. Whatever power you think you have over me, you can forget it. I'm going to open my shop and if you try to stop me I'll stab you with the nearest tree branch."

"Stop you? I wouldn't dream of it. No, I have a favor to ask of you."

Right. As if vampires asked favors. I sat on the edge of the fluffy bed and ran my hand over the high thread count linens. I would have agreed to almost anything to be allowed to lie down and take a luxurious nap. I hadn't had a real rest in days. Hell, I could have passed out in Snow White's glass coffin if it was available.

No such luck.

I raised my gaze to hers. "Let's hear it. What's the favor?"

"What would you say if I told you the Gentry were coming back?"

The Gentry. Outside of New York they were nothing but stories. Legends. A lost dream no less dangerous for being beautiful. Like the Blessed, they were forever bound to stay on the island of Manhattan, and their true name could never be spoken aloud.

The fae.

I stared at her. "That's not possible. The One Hundred Year Peace locked them away." I did a quick calculation. "We're, what, fifty years into it by now? I wasn't even born when all that went down. What does this have to do with me?"

"Your grandmother completed the spell that sealed the One Hundred Year Peace."

"What?" The One Hundred Year Peace was one of the greatest magical agreements of the twentieth century. When the war between the vampires and the fae showed no sign of stopping, the elemental witches brokered a peace: The Blessed agreed to stop converting new Initiates, and the Gentry retreated into their own realm for a hundred years.

"I see she never told you."

Defensiveness wrapped around me like a too-short towel. "My mother didn't want me mixed up in all that. I was sent to New York every summer to learn magic, not get involved in drama."

"I'm not sure I would describe it as 'drama.'"

"No? What would you call the Blessed and the Gentry trying to murder each other?"

Victorine did not look amused. "The spell was placed on a special mirror, a connection between our world and the realm of the Gentry. The Mirror Seal." The red in her eyes flared. "It is more than 'drama.' The Mirror Seal has *cracked*."

I put my head in my hands. "Oh, my God."

"Now you understand."

I understood. I understood that I left my whole life behind—my funky Florida bungalow, my job as a chef in someone else's restaurant, my car, even—for the chance to reopen my grandmother's shop. The chance to carry on her legacy, to be my own boss for once, to start over in the summer city of my childhood. And now a vampire wanted me to drop everything and stop a *war*. "You're going to have to find someone else."

"Why? Because you are too occupied with opening a sandwich shop?"

I lifted my head from my hands and shot her a look. "Yeah. I am. I'm not here to get back in the game. I was never in the game in the first place. Why do you think I stayed in Orlando? No paranormal being in their right mind lives anywhere near there. The theme parks suck up all the magic. The closest witches are two counties away. I haven't even *used* my magic since my grandmother died!"

For a moment, she looked shocked. Then her face smoothed. "If the Gentry escape, the war will begin all over again. You were not born when the last one took place. You have no idea of the chaos, the bloodshed it caused." She paused. "Your grandmother knew. That is why she did what needed to be done."

"I didn't know the Blessed had special guilt-tripping powers." Even as the sarcasm left my lips, it shamed me. She held my gaze, saying nothing, until I finally looked away. "I just—I don't know how to fix a spell. Or a Seal. How can I even help?"

"You are your grandmother's granddaughter. I ask only that you try."

Memories of Grandma came flooding back: her white apron in the sandwich shop, her booming laugh, her long stride on the New York sidewalks, her oversized purse that ate whole countries—and, in a vivid flash, the street vendors we used to visit, and how she bargained with savvy confidence.

Grandma wouldn't have been sarcastic.

She would have insisted on a fair deal.

If she could do it, I could do it. I stood and faced Victorine. "What will you offer in exchange for this favor?"

"I will offer you a lifetime lease on your shop. For free."

My jaw dropped. The value of her offer was astronomical. I tried to think of a response, but nothing came out.

Her brow furrowed. "The lifetime lease is not sufficient? Very well. A hundred thousand dollars upon the attempt."

For a hundred thousand dollars I would have found the man on the moon and delivered him in a parade float made of green cheese. But she wasn't done.

"And I will give you an artifact, to seal our agreement. Does that convince you of my goodwill?"

Whatever air was in my lungs, left in a rush. Artifacts were extraordinarily rare and powerful. They could hardly be acquired for money, let alone as a gift.

"However," she added, "I cannot guarantee the precise... qualities of the last item. Only that it should suit your needs down to the finest possible specification. What do you say, Zelda Hawkins? Will you repair the Mirror Seal?"

"You can really do—all that?"

"I am one of the Blessed. I have had years to accumulate property and wealth. Your payment is not small, that is true, but it is within my power. You are very much like your grandmother, you know. She drove a hard bargain."

I wasn't sure if I'd driven a hard bargain or just stood there while she heaped treasure on my head.

Her red irises softened, more sunlit Coca-Cola than hellfire red. "Life is long, when your friends leave you, one after another." She smoothed the bed where I had sat, as if she was expecting a guest and wanted the room to look its best. "You should go back to the party before you're missed. We will meet again soon."

One last look around the deep crimson bedroom, then I straightened my skirts and walked out. On the way down, I noticed framed and matted photos lining the stairwell, from daguerreotypes and sepia-tone to Kodachrome and modern gloss finish. Photos that spanned far more than a single lifetime.

What had I gotten myself into?

Soft footsteps descended behind me. "Here," she said. "My card."

The white card hovered in my peripheral vision. *Victorine Laguerre.*

I turned my head and met her gaze once more. Then I took the card and stashed it in my bra, since I couldn't get to my actual pockets without hiking up the Snow White skirt like a can-can dancer.

"Thank you," she said.

"Don't thank me yet," I said, as I rounded the last curve of the staircase.

About-to-be-broken Life Rule Number One: Never get involved.

Lily and the rest of the fairytale gang were still entertaining the rugrats. Prince Charming juggled colorful scarves, Cinderella blew bubbles, and Rapunzel wielded her long braid like a whip against several kids with foam swords.

I stepped into the room, boots squarely planted. "Hey!"

Everyone stopped moving.

"Which one of you little monsters wants a piggyback ride?" Whether I was getting paid or not, I was going to give the people their money's worth—and enough little monsters rushed me to take the pressure off my fellow storybook characters.

I galloped the kids around the room. Not much different than hauling fifty-pound bags of potatoes around, although potatoes smelled better, but at least it killed time and took some of the load off Lily and company.

I took advantage of the last few minutes of the party to slip into the room with the cakes.

The chocolate and vanilla towers still stood, although they'd lost quite a few slices to the plainer knife they'd found to replace the missing one. I drew the blade through the vanilla cake first, neatly removing a slice and laying it on a plate. Then I added a slice of chocolate on top of that.

My whole existence had been divided between a childhood with magic—those long-ago summers with Grandma—and an adulthood of restaurants and the everyday realness of ingredients you could hold in your hands.

Magic life, normal life. Chocolate or vanilla.

I slid my fork through the two slices and smelled the earthy scent of Dutch cocoa and the sweetness of vanilla extract. I took a bite. Chocolate *and* vanilla.

Who said you couldn't have both?

3

After the party, our storybook crew retreated to the sidewalk. Unlike much of New York, these streets were as clean as Disney World. Leafy tree branches stirred in a hot, half-hearted breeze. I pulled off the Snow White dress before the summer sun could start cooking me like a pig in a blanket. I had on a black tank top and denim cutoffs underneath—not exactly Manhattan chic, but relatively comfortable in the blast-furnace heat radiating from the sky and the pavement.

Lily held out a share of the cash.

"Oh, no," I said. "This was strictly on a volunteer basis." I needed money, but I wasn't about to take it from the pocket of my younger relation. I held out the dress instead.

She hesitated, then pocketed the money with a grateful smile. She carefully took the Snow White dress over her arm. "Are you sure you have a place to stay?"

I clapped her on the back. "Don't worry about your old Auntie Zelda." I wasn't that old, nor was I actually her aunt, but the age difference was enough to make *Auntie Zelda* a ballpark approximation of our relationship.

"Okay. If you're sure." She seized me in a hug—surprisingly strong for such a tiny gal—then walked off with her friends, all of them still in their costumes.

I'd have snuck her a piece of cake to take back to her dorm, but Lily had celiac disease and couldn't eat anything with gluten. I made a mental note to check on the best purveyors of gluten-free bread so I could provide safe food for her at the restaurant. Sure, she had more options in New York than back at home, but it couldn't hurt to have one more.

That's what you do for family. You ease the way, make life smoother.

I headed south, on foot, toward Midtown. The gracious residential buildings gradually gave way to glass-covered towers and signs with imposing silver lettering announcing vaguely named but important-sounding companies.

Although I'd reassured Lily that I had a place to stay, I didn't. Not yet. But before I had to resort to running through my limited funds paying for a temporary roof over my head, I had one good shot.

My ex-boyfriend, Daniel.

Daniel and I went way back. We'd dated, if you could call it that, in that time of life when you're still young and stupid. Thanks to my brother's big mouth—Bruce couldn't help bragging—Daniel found out we were magical.

The trouble with Daniel was I was never quite sure if he was dating me for my scintillating personality and smokin' hot bod... or his fascination with all things arcane. We broke up and got back together several times while we tried to figure it out, like getting back on a world-class roller coaster one more time even though this might be the ride that finally makes you sick.

Good times.

I assumed he saw my occasional social media post, like I saw his, in that modern spy habit of so-called mature adults everywhere. We exchanged the occasional text message that bordered on flirtation. He had his dates and I had mine, both of us equally committed to not committing. He had relocated to New York years ago, made it big, moved into one of those high-rise buildings with clean lines from top to bottom.

Kind of like him.

I wasn't sure if our occasional texts added up to meeting in person again, so I didn't call first. He'd have a harder time ignoring me if I turned up on his doorstep. I shook out my hair, flicked my cheeks, and bit my lips before entering the lobby. The welcome rush of air conditioning chilled the hair on my head right down to my scalp.

"Zelda Hawkins to see Daniel Palmer?" I said to the doorman.

He gave me a quick look up and down before pressing the intercom button. "Mr. Palmer? Miss Zelda Hawkins to see you."

Silence on the other end.

I gave the doorman a wink. "It's a surprise visit." Understatement of the century. My romantic relationships always started in the category of Seemed Like a Good Idea At the Time, before getting refiled under Oh My God What Was I Thinking.

The intercom crackled. "*Griselda* Hawkins?" All those years and his smooth, deep voice still melted me like salted butter on hot bread. Bastard. Never should have told him what Zelda was short for.

I put on a charming smile for the doorman's benefit. "That's me."

Another long pause.

"Send her up," Daniel said.

I thanked the doorman and jogged for the elevator bank before Daniel could think too much. I didn't need him to get into the weeds about why we'd broken up in the first place.

The elevator flew smoothly upward. My ears popped before the bell dinged and the doors opened.

I found Daniel's door, raked my fingers through my hair one more time, and knocked.

No one opened.

Surely he wouldn't buzz me up to leave me hanging.

Or maybe he would.

"Daniel?" I leaned my head against the frame. "It's me." I traced my fingertips over the smooth door. Vampires couldn't truly compel someone, but they had enough charisma to tip the scale in their favor. Whatever I'd absorbed from Victorine, I wasn't above using it.

Footsteps sounded.

I quickly straightened and put one hand on my hip, model-style. The door opened—but not all the way—revealing Daniel in the gap.

There he was in a pressed white dress shirt and dress slacks cut to fit. He must have just taken off his jacket. No off-the-rack suits for Daniel. No nicknames, either, never Dan, never Danny. You'd probably get ten times more for the watch on his wrist than I got for my car. Toasted spice cologne. Well-shaped muscles that didn't need bulk to show strength.

Did I mention he was a *sexy* bastard?

I gave him a little smirk, a little head tilt that sent my hair swinging. "Miss me?"

His gaze traced me. "Like a hole in the head."

I peeked around his very solid shoulder. "Got any Mrs. Palmers in there?" Thanks to the mystical all-seeing eye, also known as Facebook, I knew he didn't. But it was a good icebreaker.

He looked over his shoulder, as if checking for imaginary wives, then met my gaze again. "Would that stop you?"

"Would you want it to?"

At that, he chuckled. Then he stepped back. His right hand, the hand with a gold signet ring, gestured me in. "Get in here, you bad habit."

Point one for Zelda.

Whatever complicated financial thing he did for a living—I never quite followed—it paid well. A sleek gray leather couch wrapped around almost the entire room. The dining table and chairs had more geometric shapes than a box of Versa-Tiles. Even the floor to ceiling windows were oversized trapezoids instead of rectangles. Everything looked edgy. Sharp enough to cut.

I was more of an eclectic bohemian, myself. Jewel tones, textured pillows, and chaos.

Still, the leather couch cradled my weight in a rather luxurious way when I sank into it. I leaned back and curved my arms over the back cushions.

He retreated behind the bar, like he needed some kind of barrier in case I decided to jump him, and started setting up glasses. "What was it you called me the last time we saw each other? A 'capitalist shill for a soul-sucking corporation'? Or was it a 'soul-sucking shill for a capitalist corporation'?"

"Daniel, baby. You *are* a capitalist shill for a soul-sucking corporation—but that's what makes you so much *fun*. Champagne doesn't buy itself." I didn't drink anymore, not since my wilder days, but the sentiment remained.

He made a sound somewhere between being pleased and being insulted. "So what brings you to the city?"

"Capitalism, actually." At that, the glass slipped from Daniel's hand and banged onto the counter. Good thing he wasn't already drinking, or it would have been a spit take. "I inherited a sandwich shop. Well, not inherited, exactly. I've been given a chance to recreate it."

He leaned on the bar. "You left those nice restaurants you were working at to run... a *sandwich shop*?"

"Why does that surprise you?"

"Do you have some kind of"—he paused for a look to the heavens and a deep breath—"business plan?"

"Sure. Sell sandwiches."

"Where is it?"

"Upper West Side, my Grandma's old neighborhood."

"What shape is it in?"

"I haven't been to it yet." I didn't share that it had been unoccupied for decades.

Daniel shook his head slowly, then took his time dropping ice into each glass. "Let me guess. You sold everything you own, rolled into town, and thought you could crash with the incredibly handsome and successful ex-boyfriend you dumped years ago."

"He *is* handsome. And successful. And"—I cleared my throat—"incredibly hospitable."

That made him laugh. "You should come with a warning label."

"'Smokin' hot?'" I smiled, sensing he was close to folding. "Besides, it's only for a little while. I just have to get my sandwich shop up and running. *Cash flow*, as they say."

Daniel ran his hands over his close-shaved head. "I don't know…"

"Come on, Daniel. All the Black Cards in the world won't buy you what I have." I flexed my hands like I was showing off a manicure. The magic tracings weren't visible to him, but he knew what I was doing. "I bet you haven't seen any magic in years, have you? Since Bruce moved to D.C.?"

He stared at me with disbelief and desire. "I thought you gave all that up."

"I did. Until today. I took a side job." I told him all about my adventure at the children's party, right down to the texture of the wood in the knife handle and the exact shade of red in the second floor bedroom. "Don't you want to see what I can do?"

I swear to God, the man bit his lip. Then he let out an agonized sigh. "*Fine*. You can stay."

I sprang up from the couch. "You won't regret this."

"I definitely will."

"I'll drop off Jester later, okay?"

"Jester? Who's Jester?"

"Didn't I mention? My dog. Won't make a sound, I promise." That was actually true. Jester didn't bark; he hid.

"You didn't say anything about a dog—"

I hustled to the bar and leaned over to plant a chaste kiss on his cheek, where there was enough stubble to add a light sting. "Thanks, Daniel. You're the best." I paused halfway out the door. "Second best, next to Jester." The door clicked shut, and I hurried down the hall.

Now that I had a place to stay, it was time to pick up the one true love of my life: Jester, the sweetest, most ridiculous miniature poodle on four legs.

4

Lily had been kind enough to watch over Jester until I got settled. Her student housing permitted pets, but not guests who weren't students, so even though she'd offered to put me up, too, I wouldn't have dreamed of taking her up on it.

Thankfully, her residence hall wasn't too far away. I found the building, checked in, and headed up to her room.

Lily opened the door with Jester in her arms.

With old-soul eyes, curly black fur, and an innocent but mischievous face, Jester stole my heart all over again whenever I saw him. Although he was in fact a rescue dog, he could totally pass for a spoiled purebred, especially when he was cleaned up. Today, his coat shined, and the poodle puffs on his head and tail were extra fluffy. He even had a red bandanna around his neck.

"Isn't he cute?" Lily said. "I gave him a doggy spa." She waved his paw at me. "Say hi to Mama!"

Jester wiggled his whole body with wild enthusiasm.

I gathered him into my arms and tousled his soft ears as he tried to give my face a tongue bath. "Who's my best boy?" I always imagined his voice as if he could speak to me: *Where you been, Mama?*

"Finding us a place to stay, buddy." I snuggled his sweet-smelling fur before putting him back on all fours. He immediately tried to eat a fallen candy wrapper, but I slid my foot over it. His one major flaw was trying to put everything on earth in his mouth. "Thanks, Lily," I said. "I owe you one."

"Anytime. You can pay me back by jumping in as Snow White again."

I laughed. "Return of the middle-aged Snow White. You bet. Or maybe the evil Queen, next time. Come on, Jester. Let's go check out our new place of business." I untangled his leash, scooped up the candy wrapper, and headed out. Jester trotted happily alongside, long legs dancing with springy steps.

On a normal day I would have been tired from all the walking. But thanks to the magic I'd absorbed from Victorine, I was practically rejuvenating every half-mile. My joints were looser, my muscles warmer, and my energy levels were flying high. I could get used to being a vampire. *Blessed*, indeed. The only catch was that it gave every living being a sort of glowing red halo. A visible pulse. In a city of millions, you couldn't help but be bowled over by the sheer quantity of life around you.

Jester didn't have any magical vampire energy, though, so by the time we made it to Central Park, I was carrying him. "Lazy bum," I said, giving his poofy head a scratch.

He snuck a doggy kiss onto my cheek.

Unlike the Upper East Side with its stately rows of townhomes, Upper West Side buildings were altogether more eclectic. Rooftops ranged to all different heights, and every building seemed to be made of a different colored stone than its neighbor. Cozy shops and old family restaurants sat side-by-side with dry cleaners, thrift stores, and gently aging apartment buildings.

Grandma's restaurant was between a shoe repair shop and a bodega.

How many times had I sat at the Formica countertop with one of her famous chicken salad sandwiches and a tall, cold glass of whole milk? How many forks and knives had I rolled into paper napkin bundles? I could still feel her settling a hair net over my hair. The way it tickled the top of my forehead. How proud I felt to go behind the counter and help slice the tomatoes.

I put Jester down. The key slid into the lock and caught on the teeth. Grandma used to jiggle it just right to get the mechanism to turn, so I tried to mimic her shimmy, which was tricky to do while Jester pulled at the leash, intent on investigating some tumbling trash on the sidewalk.

At last, it worked. The door creaked open, jangling ancient bells. A wave of dusty stink rolled out, and I fanned my hand in front of my face.

Dirt and some unknown dried liquid caked the floor. The last remaining stool sprawled on the floor like someone had shot it. Behind the counter, the menu board had lost half its letters. Grime covered the workspace to the point you could hardly tell whether the equipment was salvageable.

The only saving grace was that any food remnants had dried to the point where the rats lost interest.

The filth didn't stop Jester from wanting to investigate. In fact, it probably only encouraged him. He surged forward, eager to put his mouth on everything in sight.

"No way, buddy." I reeled him back, picked him up again, and stepped further in, bits of broken tile crunching underfoot. Everywhere I looked, I saw money. Money for repairs. Money for new furniture and equipment. Money I didn't have—at least, not until I did a vampire a serious favor.

Behind the register, an ancient piece of paper hung in a rusted frame. Although the print had faded with time, it was clearly an occupational license. The business name was listed as *West Side Sandwiches*.

Except someone had crossed through the "Sand" with a red pen.

I tapped the glass. "See, boy? *West Side 'Wiches*. Grandma was a real card."

Jester sniffed delicately around the frame.

"This is our restaurant. And it's going to be amazing." I turned and surveyed the shop again. "At least after a renovation. Or possibly a four-alarm fire."

The bells rattled behind me.

Who could be calling now?

"Hello? Anyone here?" A man's voice. Behind the filthy glass stood a youngish-looking guy with thick-framed glasses and a knitted cap, peering through the door, his hand shading his eyes. Only a wannabe hipster would be wearing a hat like that in this weather. Dude was *tall*. Had to be taller than me, and that was saying something. How old *was* he? The longish hair was throwing me off.

"Hello?" he repeated.

I moved to the door and cracked it open with my free hand. My boot blocked the bottom. "Yeah?"

"I'm sorry to bother you," he said. Not quite tenor, not quite bass. Baritone. "I'm from Columbia University. Are you the new tenant?" His gaze shifted to Jester. "Is that a poodle?"

"Yes and yes."

"I don't mean to barge in on you..." Like someone born to rank or old money, he radiated self-possession under a smooth veneer of politeness. He was already confident I would let him in.

My first and most traitorous thought was *You can barge in on me anytime*, which was ridiculous, because he wasn't even my type. Too young. Too hipster-y. Clearly some kind of useless cappuccino-drinking grad student.

Jester wiggled in my arms in a frantic attempt to get closer to the visitor. There was a face to be kissed, and he needed to kiss it.

Jester had never heard of "stranger danger."

"Calm down, stupid. Not you," I added, to the stranger.

The stranger smiled. And dimpled.

Oh, Christ on a cracker. I had to remind myself he wasn't my type, no matter how tall he was or how many dimples he had.

"I'm sure he's smarter than I am." He shifted a clipboard under his arm and reached a large hand through the doorway. "I'm Berron, by the way. Berron Smith." When he saw my hands were full holding the door and holding Jester, he reached toward Jester instead. "May I pet him?"

Cartoon hearts practically radiated out of Jester's eyes. A few pats from Berron, and the tension went completely out of the dog like he had turned into a heavy pile of cooked lasagna noodles. Jester's tongue lolled happily.

"Good boy," I said.

Berron chuckled. "So I've been told. May I come in?"

"I'll come out. I don't want to put him down in this mess." I set Jester down on the sidewalk. Jester sniffed rapturously at the stranger's shoes. "Columbia?"

He fumbled at a lanyard around his neck and brought up a name badge. *Berron Smith, Columbia University, Urban Redevelopment Program.*

"Berron? That's an unusual name."

He pulled his hat off, ran his fingers through thick locks, then replaced the hat. "My mom picked it."

The things people do to their children. "Zelda Hawkins."

He raised the clipboard, displayed it. "We're seeking candidates for a pilot program that assists emerging small businesses in certain areas—"

"Assists?'"

He scrambled to flip the papers on the clipboard. "The program provides a fund—"

"A fund? Money?"

"Yes, there's a certain stipend for allowing us to—"

"Give me that." I held out my hand for the clipboard.

"You like to cut to the chase, don't you?" He handed me the clipboard and crouched next to Jester.

Jester hurled himself gleefully into his arms.

I flipped the pages. "How did you get this address?"

"This area is my thesis. Part of my work is to track changes in the neighborhood. You popped up on the last update. We're helping small business owners restore what they have, rather than be replaced by some chain."

I liked that. Grandma would have approved. And my old neighborhood in Orlando had the same struggle: scruffy local businesses getting run out by slicker chains.

"So what's his name?"

"Jester." I continued paging through the documents on the clipboard. Looked legit.

"Hmm." When he made that sound, it rumbled. "Listen, Jester. Would you like me to help fix up your shop?"

Jester enthusiastically hopped up and down while trying to lick his new friend's face.

I crossed my arms, a tough move with a clipboard in one hand and Jester doing his jumping circus poodle act at the other end of the leash. "What's the catch?"

"No catch."

I scoffed.

"No, really." He stood, leaving Jester miles below, and took back the clipboard. "Well, maybe—"

"I knew it!"

"You have to take an intern."

He said *intern*, I heard *free labor*. "No way."

"Way."

"You're not even old enough to know that reference."

"I like old things."

"Ouch. 'Wayne's World' is younger than I am."

He laughed. "I mean, I like *vintage* things!"

I laughed, too. "That's better."

His fingers ran down the stone storefront. "There's character here." He met my gaze. "I like that."

Goosebumps rose on my skin like he'd made the same move on my spine. There was something oddly intimate about someone other than me paying close attention to this place.

He released a sheaf of papers from the clipboard and held them out. "Take these. It's all here—everything we're offering, all on the up-and-up. Our office has connections to the Department of Buildings, too. We can help smooth out the paperwork process for renovation permitting."

Jester took a flying leap at the papers and missed by a whisker. I took them and tucked them under one arm to prevent another attempt. "I'll look at it tonight."

"Of course." His eyeglass lenses flashed with the reflective glow of next door's neon sign.

It was hard, for some reason, to look away from his mahogany eyes, but a glance up and backward caught the words that had made the colorful reflection: NEW YORK LOTTO.

Guess it was my lucky day.

"Think about it," Berron said. "Call me." He made the universal sign for a phone call.

"If I had a dollar for everyone who said that to me," I said, "I'd already have enough to renovate."

5

After a shower to wash off the summer sweat, I dried off with towels so sinfully soft they were almost criminal. If I stayed too long at Daniel's, I'd be spoiled forever for paycheck-to-paycheck life. But why not enjoy it while it lasted?

I hummed the Mary Tyler Moore theme as I got dressed. As I finished, the sound of voices carried through the guest bedroom door. At first I thought it was the TV, until I distinguished Daniel's voice—and another voice I knew well.

I threw down the towel and hurried to press my ear to the door.

"This whole idea is stupid," said Bruce. Ice clinked as my brother presumably helped himself to a glass of whiskey from Daniel's bar.

Ah, my brother. Bruce had elemental air magic, like our cousin Luella and her mother, but he didn't use his magic much. Unless you counted all the hot air he spewed as a lobbyist in D.C.

I flung open the door and entered the living room. "What's stupid?"

My brother whipped around. "Zelda! Hey!"

"Don't 'Hey!' me. Especially right after you called me stupid."

"I didn't call *you* stupid; I called your *idea* stupid."

I sent a look in Daniel's direction. "You see what I have to put up with?"

Daniel raised his hands innocently.

"What are you even doing here, Bruce? Other than being an ass, that is."

Bruce tossed back amber liquid and replied to Daniel as if I wasn't there. "The thanks I get for caring about my dear sister."

I looked at Daniel. "Did you tell him I was here?"

He opened his mouth to respond, but not fast enough. Bruce was already off and running. "Mom told me. So, apparently, you quit your job, broke your lease, and sold your car? For what? A dusty old shop on the Upper West Side?"

"What's it to you?"

"I want to make sure I'm not going to be on the hook for when this crashes and burns."

I picked up a stray pillow and threw it at Bruce's head.

He lifted a hand. The pillow froze in midair, then floated sideways before falling harmlessly to the floor. "Nice try. You forget I'm an air witch." He raised the glass to his lips with a smug smile. "And you're not."

Jester trotted over to the fallen pillow and gave it a sniff.

I plopped on the couch beside Bruce and grabbed his wrist. Hard, thanks to my borrowed vampire strength. "You know what I am right now? *Blessed*."

"Ow, geez, can't you take a joke? Let go—" A vaporous swirl of silver magic wound around his wrist and my hand.

The glittery silver moved through me like a cold fog, as if it were sliding under and around the vampire magic, tiny ice flakes next to hot pinpricks. I shivered. Air currents in the room became visible, and the same pattern traced across my hands in silver.

Bruce put his glass on the table and made an impatient gesture. "All right! You stole my magic, now let me go."

I had what I wanted, so I released him. Then I channeled the air, flipping Bruce's tie into his face, mussing his gelled hair. "What were you saying about me not being an air witch?"

He brushed down his suit like I'd thrown dirt at him. "You and your weirdo powers."

"Oh, *I'm* weird? What are you, Mr. Normal?" I plucked a dog treat from my pocket and levitated it to Jasper. He eyed it, then snatched it from midair. "Why did you even come here? I don't need a babysitter."

Bruce rolled his eyes. "You clearly haven't thought this through."

"Sure I have."

Daniel sprawled in a nearby chair. He sipped his drink slowly, watching both of us.

Bruce rose and started pacing. "No, you haven't. You want to open Grandma's restaurant again, right?"

I nodded.

"You don't think the paranormals will crawl out of the woodwork looking to test you like the mutant lab animal you are?"

"So what if they do?"

My brother laughed. "You won't last a month without someone trying to recruit you, kidnap you, or kill you for bragging rights. You think *we* remember Grandma? Well, *they* remember her too."

I hated it when he was right. Especially when I'd just found out she was even more important than we'd known. "Who are you to tell me anything? You don't even use your magic except as a party trick."

"At least I use it. You've spent most of your life pretending you don't even have any. You shouldn't be here, calling attention to yourself like this. Go home. Pick up your stupid poodle and toddle on back to your dinky tourist trap town—"

He choked.

Because I had used air magic to lock the air near him.

Panic spread over his face. His hands went to his throat.

"Bruce?" said Daniel. Then he looked at me. His eyes widened. "Zelda, are you—"

"Apologize," I said to my brother.

His silver magic fought mine. My own breath caught in my lungs, unable to move in or out.

Daniel was on his feet. "He can't breathe! How is he supposed to apologize?"

Bruce, turning red, nodded exaggeratedly.

My vision blurred around the edges, but passing out on the floor was better than giving in. I held my position.

Bruce let go first.

I released his air a second later.

He gasped, then took several heavy breaths. "Jesus. What's wrong with you?"

"I'm sorry, what were you going to say?" I flexed my fingers and watched the silver air magic dance.

He backed away. "I apologize, you maniac!"

"For what?"

"For—I don't know, whatever the hell you got all pissed about. Your dog?" He shot Jester a baffled look. "Going home?"

I stood and moved to my dog. His wavy, close-trimmed black velvet fur rippled under my hand.

Jester lifted his head and licked my wrist.

I stroked his back. "I don't expect you to understand, Bruce. You never cared about your magic, not really. My magic... it *is* Grandma's. It's always been wrapped up with her. When she died, I didn't know what to do with it anymore. I stopped using it." I paused. "Until now. Coming to New York—it's like she's here with me again." Something had been unlocked inside me, something that was part of the magical energy surging through my body, part of the spirit that flowed through a restaurant that was a mess to the eye but a paradise of memory to my heart.

I glanced out the window, where the surrounding skyscrapers blocked out the night sky. "So, no, I'm not going back. I'm meant to be here. And I sure as hell won't hear one word from anyone else about my dog." I scratched Jester's shoulders. "Isn't that right, buddy?" I kissed his head. "You and me, boy."

Bruce cleared his throat. "I mean, you could have said that in the first place. You didn't have to strangle me first—"

"I'm sorry. I know this is your way of trying to look out for me."

"You've never put a high priority on your income, you know."

"I keep Jester rolling in dog treats, what else do you want?"

"How are you going to pay for all this?"

"Daniel's putting me up for a while. And I got a side gig."

Bruce frowned as if he were already putting it together. "Oh, no—"

"I've been offered a job by the Blessed. Well, *one* of the Blessed, anyway."

My brother's jaw dropped. "Are you *insane*?"

"Vampires," murmured Daniel, with a gleam in his eye.

Bruce and I hushed him simultaneously.

"Watch it," I said. "They could hear."

"Sorry, sorry." Daniel moved to the bar and began preparing another drink.

"They have serious money," I said to Bruce.

"Sure they do. Which is why they can cover it up after they drain your body and throw it in the East River." He shook his head. "I can't let you get involved with that."

"Can't? Oh, *please* tell me I can't. I could use a good laugh."

"You can't tell her anything," said Daniel. "Believe me, I've tried."

"Thank you," I said, nodding regally in his direction.

"I don't like it," said Bruce.

"Too bad."

Bruce pressed the heels of his hands into his eyes.

"You're the one who didn't want to bail me out," I added.

He lowered his hands. "Not in exchange for getting you killed. I mean, you're a pain in the ass, but death is a bit much."

"This is my circus. I'll handle the clowns. You can toddle yourself on back to D.C."

"And what about Lily?"

"What about her?"

"You don't think Aunt Belinda and cousin Luella wouldn't have your head if they knew you were involving her in this?"

"Who said I was involving her? She watched my dog and I filled in for her sick friend."

Bruce eyed me.

I widened my eyes innocently.

"Fine. But you don't even want to think about what will happen if Mom thinks you're in danger."

"I don't need to think about it, because it's not going to happen."

Daniel quietly walked between us and handed me a glass. From the sugary, peppery scent, it was ginger ale on the rocks. He remembered I didn't drink. "A toast," he said. When Bruce didn't move, Daniel picked up my brother's glass and held it out.

Bruce shot me a look before taking it.

Daniel raised his, giving me and Bruce each a glance that said *behave yourself*. "To new adventures."

I lifted the cut crystal glass. "To new adventures." The cold carbonated liquid slid sweetly down, as bubbly as the new magic sparkling through my veins.

6

The next morning, I settled Jester in with his favorite chew toy, threw one of Daniel's summer blazers over my shoulders, and headed out into a light rain. I hated carrying an umbrella, and Daniel probably wouldn't mind as long as I put the blazer back before he got home from work.

Out on the street, a breeze swirled between the buildings, carrying a welcome bit of cool relief from the Hudson River. For a late summer day, it wasn't bad at all.

When I arrived at Victorine's townhouse, the housekeeper opened the door. "Miss Laguerre is expecting you." She led me to the parlor.

I tugged on the jacket to smooth it, then entered. A three-tiered tray rose from the coffee table, and a rainbow of macarons filled each level. With the children and cakes gone, the place seemed larger and emptier.

Victorine rose to greet me. When I approached, she kissed me lightly on each cheek. Not enough contact to transfer power, but enough to smell her particular scent of violets and iron. "Welcome back, Snow White."

I took a seat. "Snow White got lost in the woods."

"Did she? I wonder." Victorine made a tiny adjustment to her silk scarf and seated herself. Trails of rainwater made lace on the picture windows behind her. She poured tea and passed me a porcelain cup.

I lifted it to my nose and sniffed. Green tea, apple, cinnamon.

The vampire covered a smile with a sip from her own cup. "I am no wicked witch, and this is no poisoned apple."

"My brother suggested you might drain me of blood and drop me in the East River."

She let out a delicate sigh. "Would you like a refill?"

"I didn't drink any yet—"

She held out her hand.

"Oh! You mean—" Right. Not a refill of tea; a refill of her magic. Sure, it had been fun to be bursting with energy and stamina for a day, and seeing the population of Manhattan through a glowing red haze was kind of fun, but did I *really* need it? Or was it like eating dessert when you were already full?

I had never been able to turn down dessert. I reached across the coffee table and took her hand.

Heat spiraled up my fingers and around my wrist. The familiar burn sank into my skin, revitalizing, glowing through me. I swear I felt my hair get shinier.

When the magic settled, I released her hand, took my cup, and tasted the tea.

She watched me. "Not poison-flavored, I trust?"

"Delicious." I set down the cup. "So. Let's talk. You want a fix for the Mirror Seal."

"And you want a sandwich shop."

"You got that right. I'm going to need some kind of guarantee—"

She rang a tiny bell I hadn't noticed before.

The maid bustled in.

"Claudette, kindly retrieve the folder from my desk." Victorine gave me a serene look. "If you had been hoping to offend my sensibilities by discussing the money first, I must disappoint you."

Two macarons later, I was holding a detailed set of contracts in my hands. I flipped through the pages. "This is the kind of disappointment I could get used to." I closed the folder, set it aside. "I see the real estate and the money. I was promised an artifact."

"Indeed you were," she replied. "But these things cannot be written down in run-of-the-mill paperwork."

"How do I know you'll fulfill your end of the deal?"

"Because I will fulfill it today."

I choked on my macaron and had to drain my cup to wash it down.

Victorine calmly poured a refill. "Did I say something to disturb you?"

"No," I said, waving my hand with an air of complete confidence that was only slightly spoiled by coughing up macaron crumbs. Stay calm, Snow White. Ask the hard questions. "Artifacts don't grow on trees. You expect me to believe you have just what I need? Now? *Today?*"

"No. But I know where to find it."

I raised my eyebrows.

She stood. "Will you follow me, please?"

"Where are we going?"

"To the conservatory."

"Is Colonel Mustard there?"

She stared at me long enough to show she wasn't a big fan of Clue, then turned away.

We climbed the spiral stairs. An upper landing led to a room floored in honey-colored wood that shone in the light of the glass-paneled ceiling and windows. Soft-looking couches and deep-pile rugs filled the space. Dozens of plant stands held white pots filled with every color of orchids in bloom.

I approached the windows. The rain had washed the air, leaving the view of Central Park saturated with a thousand colors of green. "Wow."

Victorine joined me. Her scarf had been rearranged over her hair, to shade her face, and she'd put on a pair of chic, oversized sunglasses. "Are you familiar with the North Woods?"

I followed the curves of the tree canopy from south to north. "I spent more time in the Ramble, or around the Great Lawn. Why? Is there a magical artifact in there?"

"Not exactly an artifact. A being." She paused. "The Arcade."

The Arcade. Even as a child I knew not to seek out the Arcade. Grandma had told me stories of the mysterious creature who gave away incredible treasures… but only in exchange for highly personal and absolutely terrifying prices. "That's your idea of where to get an artifact? The Arcade? Do I *look* stupid?"

She slowly tilted her sunglasses down and regarded me.

"Apparently I do."

Victorine pushed her sunglasses back into place and gazed out at the view. "You need not fear. I have paid the price for you."

She said it calmly, but she might as well have taken one of the orchid pots and smashed it on the floor at my feet.

What price could someone like her be asked to pay? All the gold and jewels and multi-million dollar townhouses in the world would mean nothing to the Arcade.

"What did it cost?"

"You would ask, wouldn't you."

"I have no social graces."

A half-smile lifted one corner of her lips. "Let us say that the bill will come due soon, and I would like to have this settled before that time."

The breeze danced outside in streaks of silver. If I threw open a window and jumped, would they carry me? It might be safer than hazarding the Arcade.

I could have walked away. Let someone else handle whatever had gone wrong with the Mirror Seal. The free rent, the money, the artifact—they didn't matter. Not really. Sure, they were nice to have, but they were *things*. You don't risk your safety for things. You risk it for *people*. If I didn't repair the Seal, who would? How would the peace be maintained?

My grandmother hadn't walked away from responsibility.

Neither would I.

"Let's go," I said.

Her hands tightened. Then she turned for the stairs.

I hurried to catch up. Adrenalin trembled my steps as I followed Victorine outside to a private car at the curb.

The rain had given way to restless clouds playing peekaboo with the sun.

"North Woods," she said to the driver.

The landmarks of Fifth Avenue slid by: The Met. The Guggenheim. Mount Sinai. My fingertips traced the leather armrest. I felt like I'd missed something, somewhere along the line. Everything was happening so fast.

When the car stopped a short while later on the northern border of Central Park, we got out and continued on foot. Pedestrians, rollerbladers, and bicyclists crisscrossed the wide sidewalks, then disappeared behind us as we entered the unpaved paths leading deeper into the trees. Flights of cracked stone steps led us around giant boulders and past a hidden waterfall gurgling into a stream.

Although it was still cloudy, the sun managed to peek through the canopy.

Sweat shone on Victorine's forehead.

"Can you handle all this sunlight?"

"It will not kill me." She adjusted her silk scarf again, as if I'd reminded her of her vulnerability.

We continued down a barely visible dirt trail that twisted like a snake in the undergrowth.

Then, she stepped carefully off the footpath and into the ferns beneath the trees.

I followed, hoping my Doc Martens didn't crush anything rare underfoot. "Did you try repairing the Mirror Seal yourself? Or maybe getting one of the elemental witches to look at it?"

She was silent for several steps. "There are those who may wish to see a revival of old rivalries. If I draw attention to this matter, they may set their own plans in motion." She stopped and pressed the back of her hand to her forehead, delicately, as if feeling for a fever.

"How did you know I wouldn't do the same?"

"You are not a New Yorker."

"Hey, now—"

"And you are beholden to none."

"Except you."

She turned her red gaze to meet mine. "You will be my champion."

"Being six feet tall with magic and an attitude had to come in handy sometime."

We kept walking until the trail ended at a small clearing studded with boulders and surrounded by a ring of trees. Instead of grass, tiny white flowers carpeted the clearing.

I eyed the innocent-looking flowers. They smelled faintly of star fruit. "What's it going to do? Swallow me up?"

"It will do nothing until we prove who we are. Then you will go on, alone." Victorine raised one manicured hand to her lips. Her canines elongated. She slid a fingertip against one sharp point.

I winced. I'd lost track of the number of knife cuts I'd sustained over the years, but that just looked painful.

She extended her hand, squeezed the injured finger, and let drops of blood fall to the grass below.

There had to be a better option than using a tooth as a lancet.

I patted my pockets. Nothing. Daniel's jacket pockets. Nothing there, either. He was too neat to leave things like handy little pocket knives in jacket pockets.

"Is there a problem?" She tilted her head. "Are you squeamish, Zelda Hawkins?"

"No! I got this." My tongue slid over my front teeth, felt the canines elongate, sharpen. A part of this magic I'd never used. Something more primal, more visceral, than any red glow or feeling of rejuvenation.

I lifted my finger to my lips, hesitated, then pressed the tip into a wickedly sharp tooth. Nicked it. Tried not to be queasy at the sight of it.

A red droplet shone.

I let it fall.

The drop of blood hit the white flowers, and a rumble shook the ground.

7

The ground and sky flew end over end. I fell, landing hard on my side before rolling to a stop facedown in what felt like cold powder over concrete. An intense chill burned my bare skin and seeped through my flimsy summer clothes. What happened to the heat? To the white flowers?

I raised my head.

Darkness. Like a giant hand had squeezed out the sun. And below the midnight sky, a vast field of white—only it wasn't flowers.

It was snow.

I pushed myself upward. A powerful shiver shook my belly. I couldn't stop it from taking over every part of my body, though I wrapped my arms around myself as tightly as I could.

I turned in a slow circle. The icy plain stretched to the horizon in every direction. No Central Park. No towering skyscrapers. Not even a hot dog cart. At least my feet were slightly less cold, thanks to my trusty Doc Martens.

"She could have warned me." My words puffed into icy clouds. Where was the Arcade? And how long would I last in this bone-chilling cold? I wished I had one of those big, quilted jackets, the kind so filled with stuffing you could barely put your arms down.

Snow swirled in patches around me, like dust devils. Snow devils? A lifetime in Florida hadn't prepared me for this.

Then, with a whisper of sound, the snow formed into shapes.

Jackets. All kinds of jackets. Thick, quilted ones. Long camel trench coats. Heavy-looking capes. Bomber jackets. Biker jackets. All hanging in midair like a magical Ice Age Bloomingdale's, sparkling in the solar eclipse light with a coating of frost.

I stumbled toward the nearest one. Seized it. It crunched—and collapsed into a pile of snow on the toes of my boots.

"What the—" I snatched at the trench coat. *Poof*, gone. The quilted coat? Fell apart at my touch.

A glowing band of cold, white light twisted around me, wrapping me in the sound of laughter, then skidded away across the frozen landscape.

I let fly a few favorite restaurant kitchen curse words, the ones you try not to let the customers hear. Even the strong words couldn't warm me up—the adrenaline that heated me was fading, leaving behind sweat that threatened to turn into ice on my skin.

Something was messing with me. But how do you fight something made of wicked laughter and cold light?

Miniature snownadoes rose again.

This time, they transformed into weapons.

There were brass knuckles, small enough to carry in your pocket. Illegal in a majority of states, capable of doing a hell of a lot of damage. Tall weapons—staves and halberds—the kind of thing you couldn't haul around without attracting a whole lot of notice. A blackthorn shillelagh. Knives with decorated blades and ornate handles.

I recoiled with a hard shiver. Give me a chef's knife any day. What a chef's knife can't do, doesn't need to be done. I batted away the weapons until they all crumbled into snowy heaps at my feet.

Another teasing band of frosted light, and a laugh that chimed like glass bells.

I stomped forward. I didn't have any idea where I was going, but it felt good to move, and if I stayed in that one spot, I wouldn't be able to stop myself from kicking the snow piles in frustration. Not a good look.

Away from the piles, I stopped. I balled my fists and released them, over and over, breathing in time with the movement. I had to get calm, though I was angry and cold and starting to get worried about getting home before I turned into a pillar of ice. "Listen up, Arcade. The price has already been paid. Stop fooling around and do what you were bound to do."

Nothing. Nothing but the white snow below me and the dark sky above. Never had the unbearable heat of a New York summer sounded more appealing. On hot nights, Grandma used to sing an old lullaby. I'd join her and make it a round.

I tilted my face upward. Even the stars were different here. I had no way of knowing where I'd gone—around the world, around the galaxy, through a hole in space and time and out the other side. This was not my home.

The words of the lullaby drifted through my memory:

Oh how lovely is the evening, is the evening,

When the bells are sweetly ringing, sweetly ringing,

Ding, dong, ding, dong, ding, dong.

Though the chill shook me, I felt peace. So I sang the lullaby, my voice lifted alone, in honor of the one who sang it to me. The tune came out rough but strong. I stamped my feet for rhythm and warmth, challenging the cold, the dark, the unknown.

Take that, Arcade.

When the lullaby was done, an icy sigh blew all around. Before me, the floating figure of a woman coalesced. Her long, crystalline hair drifted like it was underwater. So did her carved ice robes, which had long, trailing sleeves that covered where her hands would have been. Her face was so bright it was hard to make out her features, except for the piercing white glow of her eyes.

The Arcade.

Her lips didn't seem to move when she spoke: *You would command me, mortal?*

"Yes, I would. Your price is already paid." I thought I'd better clear that up, to be on the safe side.

She floated closer, and her spun glass hair curled and uncurled at the tips. *My price is only the beginning. You seek to repair the Mirror Seal?*

"What's it to you?"

If you knew what would follow if you did...

"It can't possibly be worse than what would follow if I *didn't*."

Again the bells of laughter. It was worse, in person, because her lips didn't move, and those glowing eyes didn't blink. *There will be pain. Heartbreak. Even*—the being shuddered, with fear or pleasure, I couldn't tell—*bloodshed.*

"Will there be sandwiches, too? Because that's what I'm really concerned about." I hugged myself harder. The cold was making me mouthy.

You play at bravery, Zelda Hawkins. It is a mask that hides the truth: You have never, in your small existence, been truly tested.

I opened my mouth for a smart remark, but words deserted me.

Her glowing eyes nearly blinded me. *Are you afraid?*

"I—" The frigid air dried my mouth. "I'm not stupid enough to stand here in this godforsaken frozen field and tell you I'm not afraid. Of course I'm afraid. Of my restaurant failing. Of my dog getting sick. Of my family scattering across the country and growing apart. But compared to all that, you're nothing." I stood straighter, stared right in her high-beam eyes. "I will never be afraid of you."

Her hair whipped around me. *Close your eyes.*

I closed them, letting the cold wind prop me up, my heartbeat a *rat-a-tat-tat* in my ears.

You will go where you have never been. And you will become what you never were. She paused. *I grant you your prize.*

I opened my eyes to a golden mask floating before me, sleek curves with twisting designs, shedding a misty waterfall of crystal sparks.

"A mask?" I reached for it, then hesitated, expecting it to be as much of an illusion as all the rest. "How is this supposed to—"

Before I could finish, the mask surged forward. My hands flew up, but it was too late—the golden material melted onto my face like warmed honey. I pressed my fingers to my cheeks, looking for edges to pry up. Edges that weren't there.

Wear it well, said the Arcade. And then she laughed, one more time, the sound whipping away in a great wind that pushed me off my feet. As I fell, the sky turned upside down once more.

Sudden daylight blinded me. I sprawled on warm white flowers, the scent of star fruit filling my nose. I sat up. A trace of snow melted and slid off the tip of my boot.

The Arcade was gone, and with her, the midnight snowfield.

Victorine stood over me. "Well?" she said. "What gift has the Arcade bestowed?"

"A mask." I touched my face. I couldn't feel anything, but a haze of diamonds at the edges of my vision told me it hadn't simply disappeared.

"Interesting," she said.

"Interesting?"

"When you live as long as I have, everything is interesting, in its way." She offered me a hand.

"As long as it's not 'interesting' like that Chinese curse, we're in good shape." I took her hand and got to my feet. New magic prickled on my skin.

What would it do to me?

8

Back at Daniel's, I found Jester nosing around the master bedroom. He had a knack for opening doors that weren't all the way shut. "Hey, boy," I said. "Want to watch Mama try her new magic?"

Jester wiggled out from under the bedskirt, stretched, then sat and regarded me with a tilted head.

"On second thought—maybe I should call Daniel. Letting him watch would be a good way to pay him back."

Jester sneezed.

"Bless you." I pulled out my phone. *I have something special to show you,* I texted. *How soon can you be here?*

Is this your weird way of flirting with me? he replied.

You wish, I wrote. *Hurry up.* Then I tossed the phone on his bed and regarded my reflection in the full-length mirror mounted on the wall.

I held my hands out. The light illuminated them directly, and I could see the vampire magic and air magic tracings faintly aglow in tracings of red and silver. Under the bedroom's mood lighting, dramatic shadows wreathed the contours of my face.

I moved my head slowly, shifting the play of light. Where was the mask?

Ah, there it was! Transparent crystal flickers across my forehead, eyes, cheekbones, and nose. The mask was *there* and *not there* all at once.

But what did it *do*?

Jester leaned against my knee, then looked up and licked his lips expectantly. Clearly, he sensed something new, and thought it might be fun to chomp on.

"This would be a pretty expensive dog toy, buddy, if I even knew how to peel it off my face. Not sure what it would do to a poodle. Nothing good, probably." I scooped up a stray dog toy from the carpet and tossed it into the living room.

Jester ran after it.

I returned my attention to the reflection.

This type of thing really was better not to try alone. I should wait for Daniel. Who knew what would happen? What if it had some kind of cursed effect and Daniel decided to stop for a protein smoothie on the way home?

Still, I couldn't help wondering...

When I copied other people's magic, I didn't have to think about it. I didn't really have to think at all. Touch someone for long enough, and the transfer just *happened*.

Jester poked his head through the doorway, chew toy in his jaws.

"Give," I said.

He trotted over and dropped the toy in my open hand.

"Go get it." I chucked the toy through the doorway.

He scampered away.

"'You will go where you have never been,'" I mused aloud. "'And you will become what you never were.' What does that even mean?" I turned this way and that in the mirror. Daniel's blazer wasn't sitting quite right on my shoulders, so I fiddled with the sleeves. Although I was tall, and had a respectable amount of muscle, I certainly wasn't *Daniel*. Everything about him created the ideal canvas for tailored clothes: close-shaved head, angular strong jaw, sculpted torso, well-proportioned legs—

Diamond streaks shot out of the mask, pouring over me, wrapping around my limbs, tracing me with prismatic light until I was damn near sure I was going to levitate right off the floor. Glittering light layered over every part of me.

I gasped.

Neither Zelda Hawkins nor Snow White looked back at me in the mirror.

I was *Daniel*. From head to toe, the mirror lied. My jaw—*Daniel's* jaw—dropped. I turned, slowly.

Three-hundred-sixty degrees of Daniel.

Yet when I looked down at myself, I could see the illusion layered over my own body like a glowing ghost.

Then the keys rattled from outside.

I dove through the open bedroom door and skidded to a stop in the living room as the front door opened. "Daniel!"

He froze. "What the—"

What he was seeing flashed through my own mind in a fraction of a second: A perfect doppelganger of him, right there in his own living room.

Daniel barely hesitated before one step closed the space between us, and his fist came at me like a speeding Cadillac with his signet ring as a hood ornament.

I cursed, flinging both hands up and pushing with the fading remnants of my brother's air magic. Not enough left to knock Daniel down, but enough to slow down a punch. "It's me!"

Jester barked wildly.

Daniel stumbled. That gave me an opening—I tackled his knees and sent both of us to the floor.

He struggled against my borrowed vampire strength. *Blessed*, indeed. I held him down. "It's Zelda. *Zelda*." Oh, God, how did I turn it *off*? "I'm Zelda!" The diamond streaks rushed over me again.

Daniel lifted his head from the floor, looked at me, then dropped his head back with a thud. "Jesus, woman. Warn me the next time you want to play this game."

"Do I look like—me?"

"Can't you tell?"

"I wasn't sure." I let go of his legs and crawled up next to him. We both lay on our backs, panting. I examined my hands, my arms, even lifted my feet in the air. Plain old Zelda, no ghostly image over my own skin.

Jester trotted over, sniffed at both of us, gave a disapproving huff, and went back to his toy.

"I think he thought we were wrestling," I said. "He gets jealous when he's left out of the fun."

"Next time he wants to confront his own doppelganger, he's welcome to it."

I elbowed him. "And your first instinct was to punch it?"

He elbowed me back. "What would you do? Offer it a sandwich?" He rolled to his side, head propped on his hand, his face close to mine. "What kind of magic did you use to do that, anyway?"

"It's a mask."

"Where?"

"Here." I guided his hand.

His fingers touched my hairline, and his thumb rubbed lightly over my cheekbone. His pupils were wider than normal, and he was breathing a little hard. The careful examination had desire in it; whether it was for me, or for a window on my magical world, I couldn't tell. What would it be like, to always be outside, pressing your nose against the glass?

"I don't see it," he said. He let go. Then he rolled up, stood, and offered me a hand. A gentlemanly gesture considering I'd recently tackled him.

I took it and bounced up. All that magic was making me feel younger than I had any right to feel: stronger, faster, more powerful.

Daniel motioned to me. "Use it again."

"The mask?"

"No, a panini grill. Of course the mask. Let me see you do it."

"You won't take a swing at me?"

"This time I know it's you."

I touched my face, trying to be conscious of the magic when it took hold, and summoned a mental image of Daniel to match the man in front of me.

The diamond streaks poured over me again, a sweet surge of magic and light and the tiniest loss of gravity.

Without a mirror in sight, I couldn't immediately be sure of what had happened—but when I looked down at myself, I could see that ghostlike haze again. "Is it working?"

Daniel looked thoughtful. "It's uncanny."

I peered at my arms and hands. Other than the transparent glow, they were the same as they'd been for forty-some years. Maybe a little tougher these days, but certainly not Daniel-esque. My hands went to my chest. Then I laughed. "I *feel* like me."

"You *sound* like me. Turn around."

I put my hands at my sides and turned in a slow circle. "I was able to see the change in your bedroom mirror, right before you came home. And then when I look at *myself*, I see this sort of impression of you." I stopped turning. "I wonder what Jester thinks."

We both looked in the poodle's direction.

"I know!" I said. "Give him a command."

"Why?"

"Just do it." Jester didn't listen to anyone but me, usually.

Daniel crossed his arms. "Jester, come."

Jester gnawed at his toy and acted like he hadn't heard.

"Here, boy," I said.

He stretched, then walked over and dropped the slobbery toy at my feet.

I chuckled. "Good boy. See?" I said to Daniel. "He knows who his mama is."

Jester shot me what could have been a reproachful look, before rolling over, belly up. *Of course I do, Mama. Now rub my tummy.*

I bent low and delivered the tummy scratches.

"Zelda?"

I straightened. "Hm?"

"Think you could stop being me for a minute?"

"Oh, is this weird?" I flexed into an Arnold Schwarzenegger pose.

He closed his eyes and rubbed his temples in small circles. "I knew letting you stay here would be a bad idea."

I pictured myself as myself again before he got too weirded out. The magic flashed once more, and the ghostly aura faded away. "Daniel, Daniel. It was a wonderful idea. See how much fun you're having already?" I went behind him and put my hands on his shoulders, squeezed the tight muscles. "This is new magic no one's ever seen before. You're the first to see it. Doesn't that feel good?"

He grunted in response, either to the massage or my words. Or both.

"Tell you what we'll do. We'll test it out. See who else I can pretend to be: celebrities, politicians, the sky's the limit. And then we'll order some takeout and watch a nice, relaxing movie. Like *Escape from New York*." His favorite.

"You don't even like *Escape from New York*."

"Come on, who doesn't like Kurt Russell?"

He leaned his head back and opened one eye. "I'll do it if you turn into him—"

"Easy-peasy—"

"And answer the door for the takeout."

I kept the massage going. "You drive a hard bargain, sir," I said, digging my thumbs in. "It's a deal."

And that's how movie night started out—as a nice, relaxing evening for two.

Too bad it didn't end that way.

9

That evening, I took one side of the long leather couch; Daniel half-reclined on the other. Our abandoned takeout containers adorned the coffee table after we'd made our best effort at polishing off shrimp diabla and tacos vampiros from Midtown's finest contemporary Mexican restaurant.

It was nearly impossible to keep my feet from bumping into Daniel's calves, which were covered by some kind of ultra-soft pajama pants. The couch was that short, or I was that tall. Each brush ended with me quickly pulling back and staring resolutely at the large screen TV and Kurt Russell's eye patch. "Daniel?"

"Hm?" he answered, without taking his gaze from the movie.

"What are those pants made out of?"

No response.

I plucked at the hem by his ankle. "Cotton?"

He withdrew his foot.

I pursued it. "Linen?"

Daniel kept staring at the movie like he might miss some detail he hadn't seen in the last dozen times he'd watched it.

Stoic. You had to give him that.

So I tickled the sole of his foot.

He pulled his leg away and trapped my wrist with his hand. "Don't. Tickle. Me."

I laughed and easily broke his grip. "Ooh, big scary man!"

"What about when your 'Blessed' powers wear off? What if I tickled *your* foot?"

"They haven't worn off yet. So if anyone's going to be the tickle-*er*, not the tickle-*ee*..." I blew him a kiss.

He rolled his eyes. "If it will make you happy, they're bamboo."

"Bamboo?" I scooted closer, until we were sitting side by side. "Can I touch it?"

A pause. "Knock yourself out."

I plucked the fabric over his knee. "Nice. You don't put anything on your body that isn't expensive, do you?"

"I don't even know how to respond to that." He gestured toward the TV. "We're missing the best part."

I hushed. Watching TV on the couch made both of us tense with how easy it would be to turn it off and do something else entirely.

On-the-edge-of-being-broken Life Rule Number Two: Never repeat a mistake.

I tried to focus on the movie. A darker New York filled the screen, all rubble and grime. Very different from what could be seen out the window: sparkling Manhattan beauty, any flaws hidden in the streets below the soaring buildings.

Jester lifted his head from his station on the rug. In the low light, he could have been a furry black pillow that had fallen to the floor.

The pillow grew legs. Jester stood and paced.

"You need to go outside, boy?"

He hesitated, then paced again.

"That's odd. He knows to go to the door." I got up. "I'll get the leash." I'd left it on a table near the door. When I got closer, Jester stiffened.

Then he bolted for the nearest bedroom.

I turned and met Daniel's gaze. Something was nagging at my senses.

His expression was quizzical. He reached for the remote, as if to pause the movie.

I shook my head. When he started to get off the couch, I threw my hand up in the universal gesture for *stop*.

I closed my eyes. That red glow I'd seen while walking the streets of New York was here, too, even through walls, if I paid attention. I could sense beings directly above and below us, beside us in the surrounding condos, and in the hallway outside Daniel's door.

Wait. Those two were *right outside* Daniel's door. And that was a red no human had any right to glow. The same red as Victorine. If it were a lipstick color, Chanel would have called it "Blessed Red."

I whispered a curse. The Blessed weren't known for making random, friendly after-dark social calls.

I hated it when my brother was right.

I got Daniel's attention with a wave of my hand. Brought a finger to my lips. We had to stay quiet and still, because if I could see them, they could see us.

At least I'd locked the door out of habit when I answered the door for the Mexican takeout.

Then I heard a metallic rasp, followed by a series of gentle clicks.

Someone was picking the lock. And it was happening *fast*.

On a high floor, there's no second way out. You either go out the door, or you go nowhere. Those vampires, whoever they were, would be through the door in seconds. No time to block it. Nowhere to run. And *two* vampires against one semi-magical woman and one muscular but un-magical man?

Anyone who says those odds are good is lying.

I wished I felt fearless, like heroes are supposed to feel. Instead, I felt like I was back in that icy field with the Arcade, shivering from the inside out.

The light from the TV flickered across the room. My heartbeat quickened; adrenaline was kicking in. "Daniel," I whispered. "There are two Blessed outside the door. Don't try to fight them unless there's no choice left. They would clean your clock like a Swiss watchmaker." He opened his mouth, but I shook my head. "Whatever I do, *go with it*. Do you understand?"

He nodded.

I hurled a chew toy into the bedroom to keep Jester busy, then shut the door firmly. There was no time to hide him any better.

Fight-or-flight when there's no flight to be had. I had to protect us all, and I had to do it right damn *now*.

The first thing you should do in unarmed combat is arm yourself.

Sometimes, your best weapon is your brain.

I pictured Victorine: her elegant white hair, the particular set of her features, her petite frame, her understated clothing. I kneeled on the couch next to Daniel, positioning myself behind and above him, pulling his head to the side, balancing myself with my other hand flat on his chest. All the while, the prismatic streaks of magic did their work, transforming me till I glowed with illusion.

Goosebumps raced over Daniel's skin. "What are you doing—"

"Shut *up*," I hissed, lowering my head over his neck, classic vampire-style.

The front door clicked open, and two figures glided in. The door shut quietly.

I whipped my head up, bared my pointed teeth, and leveled a Victorine glare in the intruders' direction. "How *dare* you!"

The two stopped short. Exchanged glances.

I could see them clearer now that they were in the ambient light of the TV. The taller one: a skinny young man in a long black leather coat that hung from slight shoulders. His hair grazed high and prominent cheekbones. The shorter one: a petite young woman, hair cropped pageboy-style, wearing a tight t-shirt over a short pleated skirt. Nineties alternative chic.

The man bowed, his long coat sweeping out like a medieval cape. "Lady, your pardon. We did not know—" He straightened and shot his partner a look. "Jessica!"

She dropped a half-curtsy. "Lady Victorine," she murmured. The words were right but her insolent look didn't match.

Daniel's chest rose and fell under my hand.

"We are terribly sorry to interrupt, my Lady," the man said, "but we had been led to believe we would find a certain—ahem—*woman* here."

"You were led wrong," I said, with as much ice and iron as I could manage.

"Our deepest apologies." The skinny vampire attempted to shuffle backward while still issuing small bows in my direction.

The woman seized his coat. "Stay, James." She cocked her head. "Perhaps, *Lady*"—the emphasis made her disrespect clear—"you know where she is."

"How would I know, if I do not know of whom you speak?" I let up on Daniel's head slightly, and he exhaled. "Who is she? And why do you want this woman?"

James opened his mouth, but Jessica stopped him with a look. "We are not at liberty to share," she said.

What had James been about to say? But there wasn't time to keep trading words; the longer this went on, the more likely it was the ruse would fall apart. "Then stop wasting my time. Can you not see that I am occupied?" I tugged Daniel's head for emphasis, exposing his neck further, and he let out a soft sound. Sweat slicked his skin.

"Get out, before I teach you personally how I school those who have stepped out of line."

"Getting out," James said. He backed toward the door.

His companion made an exasperated sound, like a teenager who hasn't gotten what she wanted. Then she followed him out, shooting us one last look over her shoulder.

The door shut behind them.

I dropped my head over Daniel's neck again, holding the position until I had made sure that the two vampires had fully retreated. When their unnatural glow had disappeared beyond the range of my senses, I released my ex-boyfriend and hurried to the corner of the bedroom where Jester had hidden himself. There, I knelt and patted the frightened dog. "Oh, my poor baby. Did the bad people scare you?"

"No," Daniel said, "but some white-haired, sharp-toothed woman put an awful crick in my neck." He went to the door and locked it, much good as it would do. "Are we safe?"

"For the moment." Jested licked my hand and seemed to be calming down.

Daniel crossed the room and held out his hand.

I took his hand and stood.

"What was that headlock you put me in?" he said. "The Dracula special?"

"I had to make them think they were interrupting my dinner."

"So they didn't turn us into their dinner?"

"Exactly." I tapped my neck. "The all-you-can-drink special." Jester followed me to the window. I looked down. The cars below barely moved, trapped in the warren of streets, every inch another inch closer to escape. "Bruce was right. It's barely been a day and they're already after me."

"You can't give up."

"Who said I was giving up? I just can't stay here."

"Why not? I'm not afraid."

"That's the problem." I pressed my hands into the window glass, felt my palms grow cold. "You're not afraid. For you, it's all some exotic game. Another butterfly pinned to a card in your collection of rare experiences. A private island. A limited edition watch. Magic."

"That's not true—"

"What happens when it gets too real? When it's not fun anymore? I'm *responsible*, Daniel. This is my world."

"I like your world."

"Do you like *me*? Or is it the excitement that comes with me?"

"Why can't it be both?"

And just like that, crashing at Daniel's went from Seemed Like a Good Idea At the Time, to Oh My God What Was I Thinking. I picked up my dog and retreated without another word. At least I knew one being whose love was pure. But no matter what Daniel's feelings were, it didn't change what I had to do. I had to protect him. I had to get away from him.

Tomorrow, I'd start looking for a new place to stay.

10

The next morning, I waited until Daniel left before heading down to a food truck parked outside the building. I needed fuel to kick my brain into gear. Sausage, egg, cheese, hash browns, and avocado on a bagel would work nicely.

I was all set to enjoy when I saw a familiar pair of oversize sunglasses framed by white hair and a fluttering silk scarf.

I froze, half-unwrapped sandwich in hand.

Victorine Laguerre glided through the morning crowd and stopped in front of me. "Zelda Hawkins. I have heard the most *interesting* news. Would you care to take a walk with me?"

"Wanna grab a bagel first?"

"Don't be facetious."

We turned off the sidewalk into an adjacent park. The graveled path crunched underfoot as we walked alongside a bright green lawn surrounded by small trees. An empty children's carousel sat unused and silent in a landscaped alcove off to the side.

"Apparently, the Vespers Club was all a-buzz in the early hours of the morning with the news that Lady Victorine Laguerre had taken a handsome young man as a lover."

I winced. I didn't know what the Vespers Club was, but with a name like that, it was probably a gathering of the Blessed. "I can explain."

"Oh, I'm sure you can."

"No, really—

"Eat your breakfast before it gets cold."

I ate. There is possibly nothing more awkward in the world than trying to choke down a delicious meal while a displeased vampire radiates annoyance in your direction. It almost put me right off my breakfast, but the hash browns and avocado were such an inspired addition to the usual sausage, egg, and cheese that I rallied and managed to enjoy it. After I finished, I threw the crumpled foil in the nearest wastebasket and wiped the grease on my shorts.

"And they say we are messy when we eat," she said.

I ignored the dig and confessed to what had happened the night before.

"So you thought that impersonating *me*, about whom you know extremely little, was the best solution?"

"Better than trying to stab James and Jessica with a plastic takeout fork."

"And we don't even know what they wanted."

"Me, obviously."

"But *why*? Who knew you were there? And why was it those two in particular who were sent?"

"Do you know them?"

"Yes. But we are not in the same circles. Their original Elder suffered a—let us call it a 'tragic accident'—after breaking the peace in the nineties."

"How did he break the peace?"

"He converted new Initiates."

Mental math made me realize that I was roughly the same age as the young vampire duo—except they had been preserved forever as the high school versions of themselves.

What would that do to your brain?

"They were reassigned to a new Elder after that," she continued. "Lord Prospero."

"Any idea why this Prospero would want to send his Initiates after me?"

"I do not know, but he will surely be intrigued further now that my 'lover' shares an address with you. I saw him leave the building this morning." She patted her scarf-covered hair. "You could do worse."

"I am not *doing* anything with Daniel. In fact, I'm moving out as soon as I can find another place to stay."

"Pity."

My phone rang, giving me an exit from whatever she was getting at. I quickly dug it out of my back pocket.

It was Bruce.

"Now's not a good time, man—"

"Zelda, where are you? I went up to Daniel's and you were already gone."

"Oh, uh—" I glanced around. Victorine made no move to give me privacy. "I'm in the park."

"You are? So am I. Stay put, I'll find you."

"Bruce, wait!"

He hung up.

Could I run and cut Bruce off before they ran into each other?

Victorine's lips quirked into mild amusement. "Is there a problem?"

"Zelda!" my brother bellowed from behind us.

Why, with almost two million people, did Manhattan have to be such a small town?

I pasted on a smile for Victorine. "I'm sure you have a lot to do—"

"Nonsense." She turned to watch Bruce jog up the gravel path.

He was carrying two foil-wrapped packages. "They gave me an extra one by accident," he said, holding one toward me. "You're broke. Did you want it?" He nodded toward Victorine. "Hi, there. I'm Zelda's brother."

Her eyebrows rose above the top rim of her sunglasses. "Really."

"Yup, that's my brother. He was just leaving. Weren't you, Bruce?"

Bruce shot me an *are you crazy* look. "No. You gonna eat this or what?"

"I already ate, thanks—"

"You want it?" He held it toward Victorine. "I didn't nibble on it or anything."

"How reassuring." Victorine took it and slowly peeled back a tiny part of the foil. She sniffed, then recoiled.

Bruce didn't notice. "So, who's your friend?"

I looked helplessly at my vampire patron.

"Victorine Laguerre," she said smoothly.

"Bruce Hawkins. French, eh?"

"Acadian, or Cajun, if you will."

"What do you do?"

Even I was curious about that.

"Philanthropy, mostly. I support one of the oldest children's charities in New York."

Well, knock me down with a feather. The Blessed contained multitudes.

Luckily, wealthy ladies-who-lunched were well within Bruce's wheelhouse. "Oh, yeah? I meet a lot of charitable donors down in D.C. You ever head that way?"

"I have never been able to make it to the capital, no."

"Too bad. Maybe I can send some your way?" My brother, always networking.

"By all means."

Well, this was downright chummy. Time to bring it to a close before they started exchanging recipes or something. "We really must be going," I said.

"Must you? But we were just getting to know each other." She favored Bruce with a smile before turning a less friendly expression in my direction. "We will talk later."

"I'll have my people call your people," Bruce said as I dragged him and his bagel away. "She seems nice," he observed as we continued down the path.

It only took a second's glance over my shoulder to see Victorine drop her bagel in the trash before walking off.

"She just chucked your bagel in the trash, and she's a high-ranking member of the Blessed. Still feeling confident about that assessment?"

Bruce stopped, looked back. "No," he said, in disbelief. "Really?" He shook his head. "And this is who you're working for. You know you just gave me carte blanche to say 'I told you so' a hell of a lot."

"Save it for someone who cares about your opinion."

"What happened with Daniel? Why is he texting me so early to tell me you're moving out? Did you get into a fight already?"

"What did he tell you?"

"Nothing, geez! Just that you wanted to find a place of your own as soon as you could. What're you going to do?" He waved his half-eaten bagel through the air. "Move into the YMCA?"

"They don't take dogs."

"You're screwed, then."

"I have money coming."

"From your blood-drinking friend?" The sarcasm was strong. "Not soon enough."

"You know, if you spent your limited brainpower on helping rather than making rude remarks, you might actually be useful."

He took another bite, then threw away the remainder and dusted his hands. "I gotta get back to D.C."

"No one's stopping you."

We kept going. Our path looped around to the carousel. This time, it began to turn—even though no one was on it. A recorded pipe organ waltz accompanied the spinning ride. The horses spun and spun to the blaring music. Why is it that what seems fun when you're a kid suddenly becomes creepy in adulthood?

"I do know somebody who's looking for a roommate," Bruce said.

"A roommate?" I made a face. "I like living alone. Well, alone except for Jester."

"Face it, Zel. This is New York. Everybody's got a roommate these days. Look at the rent! This isn't like Florida, where you can get a three-bedroom house for a song."

"Yeah, yeah. Who's your friend?"

"She's a fire witch. Got a nice spot on the Upper West Side. Magical security system and everything."

"Keep talking."

"She hasn't found anyone yet."

"Does she murder people and make them into pies?"

"Where do you *get* these ideas?"

"Broadway musicals. Just wondering *why* she hasn't found any-one yet, what with the rent prices and all."

"She's something of a character."

"What does that mean?"

"At least look at the building. You might like it." He checked his watch. "I have time to run up there before I head back."

I watched the carousel spin to stop. You had to get off somewhere, even if it wasn't where you started. "Fine. Let's go."

We took a train from Times Square to 86th Street. A great arch inside the 86th Street station had *Excelsior* emblazoned on one side and *E Pluribus Unum* on the other. Outside, we passed a children's park with a vividly painted Western-themed mural, a metal Conestoga wagon, and concrete buffalos and cows sized for kids to climb on. A block or so from the station, we entered a narrow, tree-lined, one-way street. Like everywhere else in the Upper West Side, scaffolding that never seemed to go away lined both sides of the street.

We stopped in front of a smaller building sandwiched between the larger ones like a slice of cake stuck into a shelf of dictionaries. It couldn't have been more than twelve feet wide.

"Pretty," I said, taking in the red and white stone facade and the green turret on top. "Looks like a skinny castle. I like the green stuff on the turret thingy."

"Green stuff? Turret thingy?" Bruce said with disgust. "You don't even know what you're looking at. This is classic Beaux-Arts, you rube. That 'green stuff' is real copper. Those are Ionic columns—"

"Thank you, *Architectural Digest*. I don't have to know what it's called to know I like it. So this is it?"

"This is it. This is Poppy's."

My eyes widened. "The whole thing?" Though the building was narrow, and shorter than the ones on either side, there were several floors and lots of windows.

Maybe having a roommate wouldn't be so bad after all.

11

Bruce dusted off his hands. "That takes care of that. I'll send you the contact info and Mom'll be off my back."

That reminded me of the phone call I had meant to make. "Don't worry about Mom. I'll talk to her."

He wasn't listening. He swiped and tapped at his phone until mine dinged in my back pocket. "Sent. I'll be going now."

"Wait a minute—why are you in such an all-fired hurry to go? D.C. isn't *that* exciting."

"No, I mean, my job here is done." He grinned.

"That stupid car-salesman look doesn't work on me. What are you not telling me?"

"Nothing." He wouldn't meet my eye as he waved wildly at an approaching cab. The cab stopped, and Bruce very nearly sprinted to it.

"Bruce?" I called.

"Good luck!" He waved and hopped in. The door slammed shut.

"What are you not telling me?" I repeated as the cab lurched into motion. Then I turned back to the building. I hadn't noticed the winged stone cat perched above the doorway. The cat posed with its wings curved and folded back, its paws firmly planted on a stone ball.

It might have been staring at me.

I took out my phone and opened the message from Bruce. It contained a name—Poppy Spencer-Churchill—and a phone number.

The top half of the front door had a window and frilly cafe curtains. "Seems friendly enough," I said. "The worst she can say is 'no,' right?"

I ran up the steps and knocked.

From within the building, a slow, deep *woof* sounded. Clattering, heavy paws thumped closer. *Woof. Woof woof.*

What did she have in there, a St. Bernard?

Then, a woman's voice: "Georgiana! Georgiana, down. Georgiana, sit! Sit!"

The walls rattled as something heavy crashed into them. Behind the lace curtains, two large shadows wrestled.

"I'll be right there," the woman called. Her voice was round, bright, and British.

The door swung open.

A colossal Irish Wolfhound lunged vigorously at the end of a taut leash. A middle-aged woman, surprisingly almost as tall as me but a bit broader across the shoulder and hips, held the other end of the leash. She wore a bright red cardigan layered over a patterned blouse and slightly flared slacks. "Georgiana!" she said to the dog. "So sorry. She's not normally like this. Well, she is, but we're trying *very* hard, aren't we?" She thumped the dog's massive flank, then held out her hand. "I'm Poppy Spencer-Churchill. And you are—"

"Zelda Hawkins—"

"And you're here about the house? How totally lovely! Won't you come in?"

"How did you know I was here about the house?"

"Please, come in, come in. We can have a spot of tea. I love that, don't you? A 'spot.' Such a good word."

Georgiana dragged her down the hallway.

"Follow me!" she called, waving merrily with her free hand as she stumbled away.

I followed, shutting the door behind me.

For such an old-fashioned exterior, the inside was actually quite modern. The walls were painted a warm white and decorated with relentlessly cheerful sayings like *Choose Happy* and *Such Fun*. The entrance hall table held a basket of fruit—with a pair of craft googly eyes stuck to each piece—and the hall runner was a plush rainbow.

I entered the kitchen. Octagonal white tiles decorated the walls, accented with black and white cabinets, and clear glass jars holding cereal and pasta on a countertop of cookies-and-cream stone. A breakfast table was squeezed alongside one wall. Poppy seized a sugar bowl with such enthusiasm that sugar spilled over the edge and onto the floor.

Georgiana happily went to work cleaning it up.

"Sit. Sit, sit, sit," said Poppy, as she hastily gathered more tea things. "I just got this marvelous babka from the bakery. Do you like chocolate? Of course you do." She unboxed a loaf sized for serving six, and cut it in half. Then she loaded one half on a plate and put it in front of me accompanied by a real silver fork.

Did she expect me to polish off a pound of chocolate babka? I lifted the fork gamely, but she swept the plate away.

"It's too much, isn't it." She looked so concerned that I suddenly felt guilty. "I so *rarely* get visitors that I get so *excited*—isn't that right, Georgiana?"

I mean, I talked to my dog, too, but Poppy seemed like she may not have talked to anyone else.

Poppy whirled around from where she had been cutting the babka half in half again. ""A *poodle*! I *love* poodles! How marvelous!"

I blinked at her. "Wait. How did you—"

She put one-fourth of the loaf in front of me. "I can't help it, you see. I try, and I try, but"—here she threw her hands up in the air—"there you have it."

"You can't help what?" I knew some fire witches could read minds, but they actually had to make an effort at it. And it wasn't considered ethical to browse around someone's head like it was a Macy's.

"I can't stop it. I mean, I can't turn it off. Everywhere I go—to the coffee shop, walking Georgiana, to the movies—there they are, everybody's thoughts, like picture postcards." She sat across from me with her piece of babka. "Now, I know what you're thinking—I mean sometimes I *literally* know what you're thinking, but you know what I mean—that you couldn't *possibly* live in a house where someone sees your thoughts."

Her earnest look was the only thing that kept me from bolting. "That had occurred to me."

"But, you see, I don't hear thoughts. Not like 'What shall I have for dinner today?' or 'I think my husband's cheating on me!' I might see a great big roast beef. Or your theoretical husband *in flagrante*, if you know what I mean. And really, when you've seen it all, from the most *terribly* boring to the most *awfully* awful, you just don't care anymore. It ceases to matter."

I took a bite of the babka, chewed it carefully before speaking. "It probably matters to the people whose minds you're reading."

"I *know*. That's why I stay at home so much. But it's so *lonely* here, even with Georgiana, that it would be such fun to have someone around to have tea with." Her eyes widened like a puppy's. "You'd have a lovely room all for yourself, and an en suite bathroom, and a little rooftop patio—"

"A rooftop patio?"

"And your poodle could play with Georgiana—"

"Look, just pretend you're not getting bits of my thoughts, okay?"

Poppy pressed her hand to her chest. "I'm *so* sorry." Then she folded her hands on the table in an attempt to look calm. "I *meant* to say, *if* you have a lovely little doggy, *perhaps* he or she would enjoy the company of Georgiana?"

I put my forehead in my hand and took a deep breath. Surely no amount of reduced rent was worth this. "Show me the room."

She shoved back her chair and galloped up a nearby set of stairs with Georgiana on her heels.

I took the stairs more slowly, holding on to the smooth, dark wooden banister.

"Right this way," said Poppy, flinging open a door and letting me go first.

I stepped into a jewel box. Bold midnight blue walls around a wooden bed with carved miniature posts rising from each corner. A fireplace in the corner framed with white stone and polished brass. Built-in bookshelves holding the complete works of Jane Austen. Delicate watercolors of New York landmarks hanging on the walls in pretty frames.

"We'd be on different floors, you know. I can't hear you in here, or—or see your thoughts." She looked down, as if faintly embarrassed. "Once you're a little distance away, it all fades out. So you'll have complete privacy. Oh! And the patio," she continued, gesturing to a tiny pair of French doors.

I turned the curved handles and stepped through.

The patio was barely large enough for both of us, but what it lacked in size, it made up for in aggressive charm. White Christmas lights hung in neat zig-zags over a tiny wrought iron cafe set with multicolored outdoor pillows. An assortment of fragrant herbs filled glazed ceramic pots decorated with painted lemons, leaves, and deep blue accents.

"I'm sure we'll be *such* friends—it would only be fair to give you the *friend* price." She whispered a far-too-low number in my ear. "Will that do? It's not too high, is it?"

The mental math kicked in immediately, and it looked very good. Plus, having a fire witch on hand would be incredibly handy—*I* could be a fire witch, too. And I was already picturing Jester curled up in that beautifully upholstered side chair by the window.

"You'll take it!" Poppy cried delightedly. "Oh!" She put her hands over her mouth and blushed.

I didn't bother to chastise her.

It would have been like yelling at a sunbeam.

12

When I let Victorine know where I'd be staying, she immediately sent a car to collect me. Our earlier discussion hadn't been enough, and she was already fulfilling the promise to finish our discussion later. If Victorine was any example, the Blessed seemed to have a sense of entitlement greater even than the restaurant customers who show up at five minutes to close and demand a full meal.

Poppy waved enthusiastically from the front door as I got into the black SUV.

I returned the wave, then saw a familiar pair of dark sunglasses in the rear view mirror. "You drive?" I said.

"I've had many years to pick up skills, Zelda. Why would I not drive?"

"I guess I never thought about the Blessed having driver's licenses."

"Who said I had a license?"

Well, that settled that.

"Besides," she continued, "it allows me to keep an eye on the city. I cannot rely on outside intelligence for everything."

"You relied on it to find out about my visit from James and Jessica."

"You only prove my point." Victorine navigated one of the roads that crossed Central Park. "It is far too little information to go on."

When we arrived on her street, she brought the car to a stop and tossed the keys to her driver, who was waiting for her by the house. "Come along," she said to me. "We have work to do."

I followed her in, but instead of into the parlor, or up the spiral stairs to the red bedroom or the conservatory, we went to a second staircase that marched steeply downward. "What do you have down here? A murder room?"

"Not unless you manage to annoy me further."

A rack along one wall held slim swords with plain handles and matching daggers. Large mirrors covered another wall of the windowless room. Thick but resilient mats lined the floor.

Actually, *murder room* wasn't that far off. "A martial arts studio?"

Victorine removed her silk scarf and hung it on one of a handy row of hooks. She selected a sword from the rack, extended it, swiped it in a figure-eight, then took up a ready stance. "Defend yourself."

I held up my hands, backpedaled. "Hold on a minute. I'm unarmed. What am I supposed to do, throw subway tokens at you?"

"Those were discontinued twenty years ago."

"My MetroCard, then?" I backed away and bumped into the mirror wall.

"That wouldn't do much damage, would it?" She brandished the weapon. "Come on, then. I know the Arcade gave you something. Use it."

"It's not really in the blocking-pointy-objects category."

She lunged. "Think!"

The blade nearly parted my hair.

I dodged away from the strike, toward the center of the room. "Watch it!" This was not a fun game.

"If you'd copied your new roommate's magic, you wouldn't be in this predicament. You'd have thrown a fireball at me by now." She edged closer, the tip of her sword making tiny circles in the air.

"You can't just demand magic from your new roommate. It isn't polite."

"Ah, but you already told me you have no social graces." She circled me. "Fear concentrates the mind wonderfully, so they say. Do you find it concentrating yours?"

Concentrating? No. Making me mad? Yes. What right did she have to push me around? She wanted a favor from me, but wanted to put me in my place first? No way. I couldn't give her the satisfaction. She would respect my abilities, or I would walk, and to hell with the consequences.

Grandma would have done the same thing.

Wait—

Grandma.

Every memory conjured itself at once, like a riffling pack of cards. But I didn't even have to see the images to feel them, to feel *her* in my bones, her legacy not only magic but every shared meal, every strong hug, every lesson learned.

Grandma.

Streaks of prismatic magic washed over me, and a glowing overlay lit my whole body. The mirror was behind me, but I didn't have to see the result to know it for what it was. I had only to look at Victorine's face. At her sword, which clattered to the floor.

"Mon Dieu," she said. "It is her." She stepped closer. Her hands hovered, as if she might touch my arms, or my face. "How is it done?"

"The Arcade."

"But how?"

"I don't know. It *was* a gold mask, and now I can't take it off."

"How curious." She stepped back, to give me room. "Please. Stand here."

I stepped to where she indicated.

"Can you be anyone?"

"So far I've been my ex-boyfriend, a young Kurt Russell, you, and my own grandma."

"What about the nighttime visitors?"

"James and Jessica? I hadn't tried."

"Try."

I pictured the young woman: petite, short hair, tight top, school-girl skirt. The particular sly, insolent set of her lips. Heavy-lidded, appraising eyes. Eyebrows more plucked than the current fashion. The diamond swirls of magic flew around me again.

Victorine circled me. "Yes, yes," she murmured. "You have captured her even better than you know, I suspect. It must be a particular aspect of this magic."

"But what good does it do?" I looked down at myself doubtfully. "I mean, it's great for Halloween—"

Victorine waved my words away. "This is far better than any enchanted weapon. This is a masterpiece of disguise. Do you not understand? You can be *anyone*. You can go *anywhere*."

I turned to face the mirror. Jessica looked back at me.

"Think of it: What would James say to 'Jessica'?"

"'Yes, ma'am, may I please have another,' probably."

Victorine frowned. "Even you can see the possibilities."

She was right; I could. You could get people to talk to you, thinking you were someone they trusted. You could do things disguised as someone else to *break* trust. You could start fights, sow suspicion, steal secrets, seduce...

An artifact like this could cause an unbelievable amount of chaos, if you knew how to exploit it.

I activated the magic and returned to my normal appearance. In my mind, I replayed the conversation between the two nighttime visitors. "James seemed more respectful of you than Jessica. Any idea why?"

Victorine gracefully retrieved her sword from the floor and returned it to its rack. "The Blessed are expected to be gracious to one other. It is counterproductive to a long life to nurture grudges. However, this—like any other peace—only lasts until one side no longer upholds it. Our friend James appears to be upholding it. His colleague is not." She paused and examined a dagger. "Perhaps there is some difference of opinion between them that can be exploited."

"I can't just pretend to be Jessica, though—as soon as they actually talk to each other, they'll figure out they've been tricked."

"You'll be long gone."

"Maybe. But this game can only be run a few times before people start to catch on. It might be better to save it for something important."

"That is a surprisingly intelligent statement."

"Don't tell me you're impressed—you don't want me getting a big head, do you?"

"I could always cut you down to size if I needed to." She drew two throwing knives from the rack and turned them this way and that to catch the light.

"And you say I make too many jokes."

She shot me a look. "I believe I have a solution."

"To the jokes?"

"To the question of how to use this magic."

I crossed my arms and waited.

Victorine took two knives to the center of the floor and moved into a dance-like series of slashes. "Who sent Jessica and James? And why?" The slashing changed direction with a barrage of delicate strikes. Her movements shifted so quickly it was hard to follow where she was going next. "To do this, you will need to move freely in the community. You cannot pretend to be Blessed, not for long—we are all trapped on this island and known to each oth-er—but, disguised as a visiting witch, you can enter many of the same places without too many questions."

"Undercover, you mean."

She turned and flicked her hands toward a target across the room. The knives spun rapidly through the air before hitting the target with a stereo *thunk*. "Undercover."

My mouth fell open. "Where did you learn to do that? Your Elder?"

A faint smile lit her ageless face, as if she was remembering some-thing pleasant. "Hardly. I killed him." She pulled the daggers from the target and carefully replaced them in the rack. "Where would you like to start?"

"What about that Vespers Club you mentioned? Seems like a hotspot."

"I will find out where they will next meet."

I regarded myself in the mirror as Victorine looked over my shoul-der.

It was easy to turn my hair honey blonde, bell pepper orange, even pink like one of Victorine's macarons. I could change appearance as simply as I could run my fingers through my graying locks. I had been plain Zelda Hawkins all my life—but there would never be anything plain about my life, ever again. Who was I?

And in command of all this magic, what would I become?

13

Poppy squealed with delight when I returned with my belongings and my dog. "Oh, good Lord! How positively adorable!"

Jester hopped up and down on his back legs, enthusiastically giving her and Georgiana as many kisses as he could land.

Georgiana investigated Jester with many sniffs, and after a single, gruff *woof*, seemed pleased with her new playmate.

"Treats!" cried Poppy. The three of them cavorted down the hall, Jester leaping merrily with all the excitement. "I'll bring him to your room when we're done," Poppy called.

"Thank you," I called back.

I took the stairs and deposited my bags on the bed. My well-worn copy of *Kitchen Confidential* went straight onto the nightstand, and I took a moment to look around the room again, now that it was mine.

I could have second-guessed my decision to take this housing, but the room itself told me why I had done it. Every decorative touch spoke of good humor, appreciation of simple beauty, a lighthearted whimsy that seemed in tune with Poppy herself. It was hard to imagine how she stayed so upbeat when she had what I would have considered to be the worst kind of curse. Yet she seemed to brim with joy. No wonder she got along so well with dogs—they're nature's most uncomplicated beings, always ready to greet a new day as if every day were the best day ever.

I opened one of the bags and pulled out a binder. Inside, along with hand-written pages of expense calculations, lists of things to do and buy, and sketches of possible restaurant configurations, there was a plastic sleeve containing a single folded page yellowed with time. I slid it out and carefully unfolded it.

Grandma's original menu.

The top of the page read, "West Side Sandwiches." Three columns listed an array of sandwiches, daily specials, beverages, and Grandma's famous potato salad.

Grandma had opinions on potato salad. There were two schools of thought on which kind of potatoes to use. Red potatoes: the smaller, denser potato, with skins that tended to stay intact after boiling; or russets, the larger, fluffier potato, with skins that tended to fall off after cooking. You could make potato salad with red potatoes, that was true. But the mixture tended to separate more easily, and the potato pieces had a squeaky, tight texture. Russets, on the other hand, required a gentle touch, but the flesh was tender and the starch gave the sauce a thick, hearty structure.

Obviously, I was on Team Russet.

I placed the menu back in its sleeve and closed the binder. There would be time for more menu dreams later; for now, I needed to get my boots on the ground at the restaurant. I went downstairs and gave Jester a farewell snuggle, then headed toward the past and future home of West Side Sandwiches. A quick stop at the bodega next door yielded spray cleaner and a box of heavy-duty garbage bags—and a jar of pickles, because Grandma always said a sandwich shop wasn't complete without a jar of pickles.

Berron was supposed to meet me there soon, but I didn't need to wait for him in order to get started. Everything that was trash or unusable went into the garbage bags. I cleared away the countertops as much as possible, then wiped them down with rags I tore from the unsalvageable curtains. I swept the floor with an ancient broom I found in a corner; when tiles came loose, I threw them in an old bin in case I could stick them back down later.

I was lying on my back inspecting the undersides of the fixed bar stools when the bells on the door jangled.

Berron entered and removed his knit hat, letting a tangle of black locks free. A black t-shirt fitted his form above distressed gray jeans. "Don't get up on my account," he said.

"I was seeing if the hardware was rusted through or not."

He leaned down. "What's the verdict?"

"I think the seats can be removed and re-upholstered for pretty cheap."

"May I?"

I sat up and scooted over.

With surprising grace for such a tall, rangy guy, Berron lowered himself and laid all the way down, heedless of the dusty floor. Long fingers danced over the seat hardware. "I think you're right." He sat up. "Show me the rest."

I walked him through the front of the restaurant. "These cabinets are metal, not wood, so they should be usable with some cleanup. The bar countertop is Formica, which is practically indestructible by itself, but it's glued to old particle board, which isn't. That whole piece probably has to go. Same problem with the tables. The chairs, I don't know if it's cheaper to replace them or fix them." I moved to the back area. "The fridges and the glass case are a total loss. So's the meat slicer. And those aren't cheap."

Berron pushed a button on the ancient cash register, which issued a tinny *ding*, but didn't open. "And you're going to need somewhere to put the money."

"Yeah, it's not all going to fit in my bra." My hand flew to my mouth. Why had I said that?

Berron chuckled. "No, it isn't." He reached for his back pocket and took out a tiny notebook, the kind cops carried on old TV shows, and a pen. He scribbled down a few things. Although I tried to read them, his handwriting was utterly illegible. Then he closed the notebook and put it away again. "Okay," he said, "here's what I'm thinking. Feel free to shoot me down, you know—I'm not here to tell you what to do, I'm just here to help you make your vision come to life."

There was something pleasant about a handsome dude promising to make my vision come to life, even if he wasn't my type at all. I hopped up onto the countertop and leaned back, ready to listen.

"First off: reclaimed wood. We use it to re-top the bar and the tables. Second: vintage vinyl. You would not believe the stuff that's out there. Old auto vinyl for a song. Got that retro vibe and everything. Totally new seat cushions all around."

"Keep talking."

"We keep the tile. Any missing bits, we can cut them ourselves. Chair frames and table legs get the rust removed. Do you have a budget for the equipment you need?"

I nodded.

"I'll call around to the secondhand restaurant depots. They get everything usable when places go out of business."

I jumped down. "I like it. Let's do this thing."

Berron unpacked two drills from his bag and we set about disassembling the tables and chairs. The bar took a lot more contortion from both of us, but we managed to get it free and lug it over to the wall to prop it up out of the way.

By the time we had finished with all the manual labor we could handle for one day, we were both drenched in sweat and covered in a layer of grime.

Berron pushed his hair back and laughed. "I must be a sight."

I leaned against the countertop. "No more than me." I rummaged in my bag for cash. "Listen, let me buy you a Gatorade or something from next door. It's the least I can do."

"You're too kind."

"I insist."

"I'll tell you what—I'll buy the next round. Deal?"

I high-fived him.

We left the shop behind and entered the bodega.

A white cat with dark pointed ears had draped itself over the potato chip stand. It raised its head sharply when we walked in and let out a piercing meow, halfway between a growl and an electric weed whacker. The potato chips crackled as it shifted position.

Berron reached for the cat.

"Be careful. He bites," said the man behind the counter, without raising his head from the paper.

"Does he?" Berron replied, scratching the cat under the chin.

"Well, usually he does."

The cat jumped down from his chip throne and followed us to the drink cooler. I grabbed something cold and blue. Berron picked a bubbly water. Then we headed back to the counter.

"So you found her," the man said, ringing up the drinks.

I looked at Berron. "You found me?"

"He was in here a few weeks ago, looking for the owner of that old sandwich shop next door."

"That's me."

The man cast me an appraising look. Then he nodded. "It's good to have it occupied. Better for business." He slid the drinks across the counter. "Have a good day."

I wished him the same, and we left.

We followed 81st Street due west past old apartment buildings with canopied entrances, across the wide intersection with Broadway, down to the curve of Riverside Drive, and into Riverside Park. The breeze off the Hudson River dried some of my sweat.

"My Grandma and I used to come here sometimes," I said. "Although she preferred Central Park."

"Any particular reason?"

"She said Central Park at least made an effort to look wild. Riverside was too manicured for her taste."

"I have to agree with your grandmother. I mean, there's something to be said for the open views, but... I like the idea of being a bit lost. Trees all around. A waterfall in the distance. Birds hidden in the branches. I even like how the sunlight loses its power under cover of the leaves. Can you imagine what it must have been like here before all the buildings?"

We both stopped, taking in the view.

Instead of sidewalks and stately white fountains, I pictured thick forests, great trunks of trees, a canopy so thick the early evening would become the edge of night. "And yet you've dedicated your career to restoring buildings."

Berron smiled, almost to himself. "Restoration is my *jam.*"

I laughed. "Any 'jam' I have goes on sandwiches."

"I'm glad our jams align."

In the golden light, with the wind tumbling his black hair into tangles, he looked older than I first thought. Which was ironic, because spending time with him, even in the dirt and grime of cleaning, made me feel younger than I had in years.

14

When I woke up the next day, there was nothing I wanted more than a conversation with my mother.

There was also nothing I wanted less.

It wasn't that Mom and I didn't like each other. In fact, we had a kind of fierce appreciation for one another. We were both opinionated. Both sure we knew what we wanted.

It only hit the fan when we wanted different things.

She'd been successful by going to college, becoming every inch the professional librarian, rising to the head of her department at the local university. I'd been successful by going straight into cooking after high school. Hospitality classes—at least the ones I maybe could have afforded—were filled with sleepy burnouts and starry-eyed career-changers who didn't know a stock pot from a saute pan. It didn't make sense to throw my money away on a piece of paper that wasn't going to net me as much profit as putting in the time in a real kitchen.

And there I was, having the argument in my own head, no mother needed. Funny how you learn to do it all by yourself.

I sighed and found an empty seat on the train. Thanks to spotty or nonexistent phone service on the ride down to Lower Manhattan, I could avoid making the call for a few more minutes.

I hadn't done much of the touristy things in years, and this seemed like the perfect opportunity to clear my head and take in the view of Manhattan from the Brooklyn Bridge.

Sometimes you have to be outside something to appreciate it best.

I emerged near City Hall Park and made my way past colorful art installations to the entrance to the bridge. The air carried the smell of sea salt and diesel smoke. Behind me, skyscrapers towered over older buildings. The Brooklyn Bridge stretched like a great arm across the East River, its ligaments made of steel, its cuffs of stone.

I pushed the dial button on my phone and began the crossing.

My mother answered. "Hello?" Her voice had that touch of Southerness like a candied flower on a salad: sweet at first bite, but with crisp, no-nonsense greens underneath and a splash of vinegar on top. God help the person who tried to put one over on Effie Hawkins.

"Hi, Mom."

"How are you? Did you find a place to stay? Bruce said he was helping you."

Siblings always report back, and they always take more credit than they deserve. "Yes, Mom. I have a place now."

"And the restaurant? Is it coming together?"

"May take a few weeks to get up and running."

Ah, small talk. If we'd been honest, it would have been more like *I think your plan of dropping everything to move to New York is crazy* versus *Well, I think it's a great adventure*, and we would have gotten nowhere at all.

"Listen," I continued. "I gotta ask you some things about Grandma." I knew the rules. You didn't discuss anything magical over the phone or on paper. But I needed any information I could get, even if it was in a roundabout way.

"Oh?" It was amazing how she could communicate so much with one syllable. Although Mom tolerated all the magic in the family, she treated it like having a bunch of relatives who played the kazoo on street corners for loose change. Harmless but not entirely respectable. "Where are you? What's all that noise in the background?"

And there was the stealthy Southern change of subject. She was good, I had to give her that. "Brooklyn Bridge," I said.

"Sounds like a circus."

I pressed on. "Did Grandma ever tell you about anything special she accomplished while she was here? Like, life-altering. History-making. *Major.*" Silence on the other end. "Mom?"

"When, exactly?"

"The seventies."

"She moved back up there when your Aunt Belinda and I were grown, after your grandfather passed. I didn't think she'd stay for good—it certainly wasn't an easy time to live in Manhattan—but she was determined to keep the old family business alive."

"Was that all?" If I pushed gently, her librarian love of sharing facts might override her natural instinct to avoid talking about magic.

More silence. Then she sighed. "Now, it's only my opinion..."

"Go on."

"But I think she was up north for some other reason."

"How do you know?"

"Oh, you know, Zelda. The same way I knew you going up there wasn't just about the restaurant."

I stopped walking. "What do you mean?"

"Was it?"

"Was it what?"

"Was it entirely about the restaurant?"

I started walking again, as if to outpace the question. "Yes..."

Mom made a disbelieving noise. "Anyhow, your Aunt Belinda and I assumed that, whatever else she had been involved in, the matter was closed when she passed."

That closed matter had been opened like a ripe banana. "Could you run this past Aunt Belinda?" Aunt Belinda lived over an hour away, on the Atlantic Coast, in a town called Sparkle Beach. "In case she knows anything else?"

I didn't have to see her to feel her feathers ruffle. "I may not have been the 'talented' one in the family, but anything Belinda knows about our mother, I know." Her feathers settled. "I'll let you know if I learn anything new," she added.

"Thank you." I had reached the halfway point of the bridge. According to local lore, the trip didn't count if you went half the distance and turned around. You had to go all the way before you could come back.

"And—Zelda?"

I waited.

"I know you want to honor your grandmother's legacy, and that's an honorable thing, but remember to be open to new things as well. I hear they have a *marvelous* writing program at Columbia."

I laughed. Trust Mom to find a way to plug higher education. "If I decide to go back to school, you'll be the first one I call."

"Now go on, I don't want to keep you. I know you must be busy up there."

"Love you, Mom."

"I love you, Zelda girl."

We said goodbye and hung up.

Cars whizzed by below the wooden boardwalk as the Brooklyn skyline grew larger. I passed under the second set of arches and continued until the wooden planks gave way to a concrete sidewalk.

I'd gone all the way.

I turned around and faced the way I'd come. Not only had I satisfied the local custom, I had done what the Blessed and the Gentry couldn't do.

Leave.

What would it be like to be stuck in twenty-two square miles? Even Disney World was twice that size. All the charms of the greatest city in the world might not seem so charming with a lifespan that ticked on and on. I mean, if you had to be stuck somewhere—forever—was this where you'd choose? An entirely concrete landscape you could walk from end to end in a few hours? I imagined the bridge rolling up, cutting off any escape. I didn't like the feeling.

On the way back, my phone buzzed once. I ignored it until I re-entered Manhattan.

It was from Daniel.

About the other evening. I wasn't as clear as I could have been. I sent something over to your new place. I hope you'll forgive me, considering the circumstances.

I read the last line again. Was he asking for forgiveness for what he had said, or for taking the liberty to send me a present? Apologies weren't Daniel's strong point. I could understand that—they weren't mine, either. Although I wanted to stay mad, another part of me thrilled with a rush of curiosity.

The midday sun beat down strongly by the time I got back to the townhouse with the green copper turret. I let myself in and found Jester waking up from a nap.

He stretched deeply—a real downward dog if I ever saw one—and trotted over to say hello.

"Who's a good boy?" I said, caressing his fluffy head.

His long tongue swiped upward hopefully in an attempt to kiss my face.

"Oh!" cried Poppy from down the hall. "It's you! There's a package!"

I headed down the hall and Jester followed. The closer we got to the kitchen, the more I could hear Poppy's upbeat music playing.

Poppy was grooving in a dance-like shuffle. "It came earlier by courier. Very posh." She opened a cabinet mid-groove and retrieved a rectangular white box bound with a wide, glossy black ribbon.

I slid the ribbon free and lifted the lid.

Poppy stopped dancing and leaned closer.

A second wooden box was inside. I removed it, set it on the counter, and opened the hinged lid.

An eight-inch chef's knife lay in the black velvet embrace of the interior.

I drew it out of the box.

This wasn't your superstore chef's knife special, with a plastic handle and a blade that would snap on a sweet potato. Nor was it a snooty Food and Wine Magazine feature, all flash and wasted money.

This was a true chef's knife. A workhorse. An *I-mean-business* blade. A well-balanced wood handle that wouldn't slip. A quiet assassin of potatoes and onions.

Damn Daniel and his really good presents.

Poppy clapped her hands in excitement. "Who's it from?"

"My ex-boyfriend."

"Oh, good Lord! Is he going to *murder* you? Should I call the police?"

I shook my head, chuckled. "No. I was going on and on about this cool knife I saw at a party. So he got me one."

"Oh, I *see*." She peered at it closely, as if it might do something interesting. "Is he in love with you?"

I nearly dropped the knife on my foot. "No!"

"I mean, I'm not trying to be *rude*, it's just that it's never a surprise for me." She nudged me. "The love, you know. Or the murder."

I carefully placed the knife back in the box. "Someone tried to murder you?"

"Not me, personally. But people think the most terrible things all the time. You'd be shocked by the average ride on the subway, I tell you. *Shocked*. It's amazing I haven't gone quite mad."

The wide-eyed smile she aimed in my direction argued that she might have been edging in that direction. But who wouldn't, if they could see humanity's unfiltered thoughts? "Listen, Poppy. I need to level with you about my own magical powers."

"You mean how you can copy witches' magic?"

I blinked. "How did you pick that up?"

"Oh, I didn't. Your brother told me."

"My *brother* told you?"

"Very briefly. He doesn't like to hang around. He thinks it's weird, my ability. Most people do."

I opened my mouth in that automatic way we have of reassuring people with things that are comforting but not necessarily true. Like when people told me: *You're not that tall*. But having even the remotest chance of mind reading makes it very hard to bend the truth.

So I simply said what I felt. "It's not weird. You can't help it, any more than I can help copying other people's magic when I touch them. You do your best to work around it. And along the way you'll find people who understand."

"Or dogs," she added, patting Georgiana with hearty thumps.

"Always dogs." I picked up Jester, who immediately licked my face.

"Now," said Poppy, briskly, with the air of someone consciously changing the subject, "how about you copy my fire magic and we make some summertime s'mores?"

I waved Jester's paw and spoke in the silly voice I used to speak for him: "Is good plan!" Then I set him down and quietly turned away from Poppy to send Daniel a message: *The knife is amazing. Why don't you watch me test it out on Monday?*

That would give me time to get the place a bit more spiffy. I had my pride, after all.

The phone went back in my pocket and a smile tugged at my lips.

15

After several days of demolition and rebuilding with Berron, I crashed into my four-poster bed in my jewel box room and stared gratefully at the ceiling. Jester leaped onto the bed and flopped into a heap beside me. Soon, my eyes would close, and I would sleep for the entire weekend. The anticipation tasted as good as sugared whipped cream. "We've earned it, Jester. Sweet clouds of blissful sleep."

Then my phone buzzed.

And that's when I received word from Victorine that the Vespers Club would be meeting from sundown to sunrise.

I covered my head with my arms and groaned. I had left late-night outings largely in the distant past. Late work nights, sure. That came with the territory as a chef: nights, weekends, holidays. But all-night clubbing? Spare me. That was for twenty-something Zelda, God bless her.

The message from Victorine included only the time and the address. I looked it up on my phone.

The vampire all-nighter would be held at a church.

I poked around for more information. The parish had been shut down due to disrepair and a dwindling congregation. Online, it was officially listed as "Permanently Closed," its status spelled out in white on a bright red banner.

I hauled myself out of the bed. Jester lifted his head and looked mildly hurt. Like, *What happened to sleep, Mama?*

"No rest for the wicked, buddy. Or—no rest for those who party with the wicked."

First things first: I checked my arms. The tracings of magic were strong; I had vampire magic from Victorine, fire magic from Poppy. I would have preferred to have air magic, and earth magic, and any other magic someone could conjure, but what I had would have to do.

Second: I checked my face. The mask was still there, tiny flickers of crystal across my skin like morning light caught in spider web dew.

As far as magic went, I was all set. As far as regular old human energy, I would have preferred to leave the partying to my past self—

Maybe that was *exactly* what I should do.

A second wind blew through me. I hurried through a shower and dried off. Sure, no one could see me if I was in disguise, but they might be able to smell me, and no one likes *Eau de Sweat*. Then I stood before the full-length mirror, comfortably dressed in a clean pair of shorts and a tank top, no makeup, and mostly dry hair.

"You're the first to go." I traced my fingers over the gray and watched it fill with color. My high school haircut, a crunchy set of bangs and medium-length hair in a scrunchie, resurrected itself in the reflection. My face became smoother, smaller, rounder. My neck looked like I had an A-list surgeon on speed dial. Everything else shrank and lifted into youthful lines.

Now for clothes.

My favorite outfit in high school was a short flared black skirt and a laced-up black chiffon v-neck over a black camisole.

Whatever else had changed, my color preferences hadn't.

I used to wear it with—what else?—black open-toed high heels. The fantastic thing was, I *looked* like I was wearing high heels, but I was really wearing comfy shoes. "If this kind of magic ever hits retail, Jester, they'll make millions."

Finally, a black choker to complete the look.

I turned back and forth to see all angles in the mirror. I should have mourned the loss of youth. And I did, maybe, but not for what was visible—I missed my effortless flexibility and lack of pain more than I missed smooth skin. The girl in the mirror, the *Zelda* in the mirror, looked so soft and vulnerable even in all that black that I wanted to give her a hug.

Instead, I scooped up Jester. He didn't care what I looked like. I was his person, and that was all that mattered. "Be a good boy while Mama goes to work, okay?"

He licked my hand.

I set him down and reverted to my normal appearance. It wouldn't be smart to be seen leaving as someone else, and I wasn't ready to start explaining it to Poppy quite yet. I'd find a spot, like

Superman's phone booth, and make the change before I got to the party.

On the train down to the East Village, tired people heading home shared the space with Friday night revelers just starting to gear up. The mood was loud, loose, and hot, as the summer heat had gotten trapped underground during the day.

Back on the street, I ducked into the closest coffee shop. Fully supplied with caffeine and transformed into Past Zelda—thanks to a customers-only restroom—I continued to the abandoned church.

The sparse pictures online didn't do the building justice. The church looked like a distant cousin of the White House. Four columns accented the smooth white facade and supported a green copper triangle. Copper turrets topped the two front corners. The stairs from the street led to three equally spaced arched doorways, echoed by two arched windows on either side, and a round window above the center doorway.

The door on the left was slightly ajar.

The church had already been abandoned. Someday they'd sell it to a developer, tear the whole thing down. When that happened, more than marble and brick and copper would fall. What spirit occupied it now? And where would it go when its home was gone?

I said a prayer to whoever might still be listening. Then I approached the door.

"Who goes there?" said a haughty female voice from the dark slit in the doorway.

"One who would worship." I'd been given the password by Victorine, who had also informed me that once inside, I'd have to demonstrate magic to avoid getting bounced or outright attacked.

The Blessed could simply show their ability to drink blood.

"Enter," said the strangely familiar voice.

I stepped inside. The entrance was barely lit. As my eyes adjusted, I saw the doorperson.

Jessica.

"Come on, witch, we haven't got all night."

Up close, it was startling how we could have gone as a matched pair to Nineties Goth Night. I managed to smooth out my expression before I raised my hand, palm up, and conjured a simple yellow flame.

"Pass," she said in a bored tone.

I held my exhale until I reached the second pair of doors, where the loud punk music covered my sigh of relief.

Even the garish red lights didn't take away from the beauty of the interior. In fact, it took an effort not to stop and gawk. Round columns supported arches leading to the altar. Above the altar, richly painted Bible scenes contrasted with the smooth white walls.

Along both sides of the church, elevated alcoves held colorful life-size statues of saints. Their expressions were remarkably calm considering what was going on beneath them.

An all-female band rocked out in the open space between the forward benches and the altar itself. Witches and vampires alike pogoed in the aisles and on the pews. Wine—or something—spilled heedlessly from cups. Two men laughed and staggered as they dueled with lit candelabras.

I slid through the crowd and found the makeshift bar tucked under the statue of a female saint holding white flowers and a book, and wearing a crown of thorns over her white veil. I didn't want a drink, but I would have looked strange without one, so I ordered a cup of the night's special and deposited some bills into a dry stone font that served as a combination till and tip jar. "Hey," I said to the bartender. "Have you seen James?"

The bartender scooped ice, poured tequila and lime juice, then stirred in sriracha sauce. She passed the cup over and jerked her head in the direction of the altar. "Try down front."

The fumes of the savory drink tickled my nose as I moved on.

The trio dominating the impromptu stage wore neon colors mixed with jet black and animal print. Each band member had a wildly different hair color: the singer-guitarist, hot pink; the bassist, candy blue; and the drummer, bright purple.

A loud and enthusiastic crowd filled the front rows. The audience bobbed, pogoed, or thrashed as the music moved them. Thank God it wasn't quite up to the level of becoming a mosh pit. I wasn't up to moshing, not if I didn't plan on visiting the emergency room by the end of the set.

The song came to a close. The bassist and the drummer gave a final flourish as the lead singer gripped the mike with one hand and acknowledged the cheers with a fist pump. "Thank you! We are the

Melee Diamonds... and we'll be back! In! Five!" One last stinger chord from her guitar and the three women stalked off the stage.

The crowd thinned out as the partygoers drifted off. As the view opened up, I spotted a long black trench coat across the center aisle.

James.

He stared at the altar like a man transfixed. His cup hovered near his lips as if it was an automatic process he had no control over. What was he thinking about?

I edged closer until I was standing next to him. I pretended to focus my attention on the altar's artwork, too. "Great show, huh?"

James barely glanced at me. "Sure."

"Are you a fan?"

"Yeah."

This was going nowhere fast. Time to turn up the charm. I pivoted to face him, even though he kept staring straight ahead. "I like your jacket."

James sighed and looked forlornly into his cup. "Listen, love, if you're flirting with me, I have to tell you—no offense—I'm not interested."

I took a sip from my cup to buy time while I recalibrated.

Dear God! That stuff would knock me on my ass if I let it. I hid a grimace and soldiered on with my best pouty-lipped young thing impression. "Why not?"

"Here, have this," he said, pushing his cup into my hand. "You seem to like it more than I do." And with that, he walked away. He pushed past the revelers and headed toward a plain door in the far left corner.

I was left with my mouth hanging open and two cups of a drink I didn't want.

Where was he going? I quickly set down the cups in the pew and followed, trying not to be too obvious about it.

In a blink, he was through the door and gone.

I paused in the shadow beneath a statue. Was it wise to pursue a vampire deeper into an abandoned church? While the party raged and the Melee Diamonds rocked, no one would hear me even if I howled for help.

And if they did, they might help James, not me.

The Melee Diamonds were gearing up again. Bass notes thudded through me, followed by shivers from the cymbals.

I needed to know who was after me, and why. I had flames at my fingertips and the strength of the Blessed in my limbs.

I opened the door and stepped into the darkness.

<h1 style="text-align:center">16</h1>

I had a choice between using my phone flashlight or a conjured flame. I picked the flame. Didn't want to risk dropping my phone, and a flame in my hand doubled as illumination and weapon.

The yellowish light spilled into a hallway tagged with graffiti. Paint peeled from the ceiling and dust covered the floor. I passed a rusting water fountain and continued on the balls of my feet, trying to make as little noise as possible.

The hallway ended at another door. This one opened into a room filled with a jumble of shelving units, some old wooden desks, and a cracked green chalkboard. This wasn't just a church. It had been a school, too. I stepped around plastic student chairs and a space heater on wheels. On the other side of the room, above the other door, someone had spray-painted the words "Carpe Noctem" in elaborate letters.

I passed through the door and into a stairwell. I stepped lightly on the wooden stairsteps to avoid announcing my approach.

Amateur paintings decorated the walls with icons of faith. Each flight upward revealed more: A jar of pouring water for baptism. A flame for confirmation. A cup for communion. Double rings for matrimony. A stole for holy orders. And above it all, a white dove with its wings spread.

At the top, one last door. I could smell outside air filtering through the crack beneath it.

The bell chamber.

I placed my hand on the knob and turned it.

The door swung open with a creak.

Moonlight silhouetted James at the belfry opening. He turned, looked at me, then turned away again. "Go back to the party."

"I wanted to see the bell."

"Lies. You wanted a little excitement. A thrilling little story you could take back to your witch friends." He scoffed. "Find another Blessed. I'm sure they'll help you out."

Perhaps I had miscalculated. "Is it because... I'm a woman?" I said, carefully framing the question with simple curiosity, not judgment.

His laugh was bitter. He whirled around and his trench coat flared like a cape. "Is it because you're a woman? No." He stalked closer. "Look at you. You're what, eighteen? Nineteen?"

I nodded.

"You think I'm some hot-blooded young guy, eager to pursue every pretty thing that crosses my path?"

"I—"

"I am, without a doubt, more than twice your age. I could be your *father*. No matter what I look like on the outside"—here he flicked his fingers against his chest with an air of disgust—"inside, I am a forty-five-year-old man who feels *every single year* of his life, who would rather be tucked into a cozy suburban bedroom with a loving wife, a minivan in the driveway, and several sleeping children down the hall, than be here at this wretched party that I will have to attend until someone finally stakes me in my dried-out heart and puts me in the ground. Do you understand? I am *not interested.*" He pointed to the door behind me. "Now, get out!"

The flame in my cupped hand burned painlessly, each flicker marking the passing of time.

You'd think he had everything he'd ever been told to dream of.

Youth.

Beauty.

Immortality.

Yet misery hung on his face like a funeral wreath. Instead of facing his teenage self with compassion, as I had done, safely, from the distance of decades, he was an unwilling Peter Pan who could never grow up.

Who would have thought that being young forever would be a nightmare?

I'd gone about this the wrong way.

I closed my hand, extinguishing the flame. My disguise faded away. I stood before him as forty-six-year-old Zelda. "James. I understand."

His eyes widened. "You're *her.* You're the one we were told to find. Zelda Hawkins."

"Yes."

"Why were you—"

"Disguised as a teenager?" I walked closer, the better to see his expression in the moonlight. If I was going to take this risk, I needed to lay it all on the line—and fast, before the situation went south. "Because I needed to get close to you. To find out why you and your friend were looking for me that night."

James made a derisive noise. "She's not my friend."

"Okay, why you and your not-friend were looking for me that night."

"Do you know what it's like to be stuck with your fleeting high school crush for the rest of eternity?"

He wasn't answering my question, but I played along anyway. "Is that what Jessica is? An old flame?"

"We never even *dated*. I had the hots for her, or I thought I did, and when some weird guy offered to turn us into *this*"—he pointed to his fangs—"I went along with it because I thought she would think I was *cool*. Well, not only does being a member of the Blessed *suck*—pardon the pun—but he wasn't supposed to be turning any Initiates, and he promptly got executed for it. Now we 'belong' to someone else, and we rank so low that we'll never be anything but his forever gofers." He kicked a wall. "Joined at the freakin' hip."

"And you want out."

"Damn right, I want out. But Jessica's obsessed with climbing to the top of the heap, even if she has to drag me along with her."

"Why were you so respectful of Victorine Laguerre?"

James did a double take. "That wasn't her, was it? That was you. In disguise."

"Answer the question."

"Because I heard she might not be as bad as the rest. I thought if I kept on someone's good side, maybe someday someone would help me."

"But there's no cure. And you can't leave even if you wanted to."

"Do you have anything that gets you out of bed in the morning?"

I thought, instantly, of Jester. Grandma's sandwich shop. My family, who could be difficult but I loved all the same. Daniel and his unexpected apology present. Berron and the way his hands restored everything he touched. Even Poppy and her massive dog, Georgiana, and my fanged landlord-boss-mentor, Victorine.

"Of course you do. I can see it on your face," he continued. "So do I. It's called *hope*. A spider-web strand of hope."

"That someday you'll have the house and the minivan and the family."

He flung a hand in the direction of the bell. "It's about as likely as that bell ringing again.'"

"No. No, it isn't."

James cocked an eyebrow.

"I don't know how to help you. Yet. But if you'll help me, I'll do everything I can to help make your picket fence wishes and minivan dreams a reality."

"You're sweet."

"I'm serious."

He looked away.

"James, how long do you want to keep living in this hell?"

A loud creak sounded behind me.

James ran to the door faster than I could react. Then he let out an impressive series of curse words. "She heard."

"Who heard?"

"Who do you think? Jessica! And now she's running as fast as she can to tell Lord Prospero that I'm going to betray him."

Suddenly, being trapped in an isolated bell chamber at the top of a flight of stairs with no other way down didn't seem like a very good idea. "We need to get out of here."

"You think?"

"Your sarcasm doesn't help." Fire magic wouldn't do us much good, either. Trying to burn our way out would attract too much attention, and could endanger innocent people. I shut the creaky door. There wasn't a single stick of furniture to bar it with. I hurried to the belfry opening and looked down. "How are you with heights?"

"Heights? I can't turn into a bat, if that's what you're asking."

"Come on." I sat on the sill. "Fire escape." This one wasn't the cute zig-zag staircase style. It was a straight up-and-down retractable ladder. I had to hope that my vampire strength extended to not breaking every bone in my body if I slipped. "Help me."

Together, we pushed the ladder down.

"I'll go first," James said.

I gave him a look.

"Not because I'm a coward," he said, "but because if I slip, I don't want to take you down with me." With that, he swung his leg over the sill.

"Wait. They already know we're here, right?"

"Right..."

"And the last thing they want is attention."

"Your point?"

I grabbed the bell rope. "This'll scatter 'em like roaches and bring half the neighborhood running to see what's going on."

"Oh, I don't know if that's such a good idea—"

I yanked the rope as hard as I could.

BONG.

Again. *BONG.*

Once more. *BONG.*

"*Now* we go," I said.

James began the climb.

I watched him get partway down before I started. I'd never been so grateful for enhanced strength, not just in my arms and legs, but in my core to keep me stable as I climbed down. Too bad it didn't stop me from sweating profusely. I gripped as hard as I could and kept going. As long as I didn't look down, I'd be golden.

James jumped off and landed in the alley.

I took the last few rungs and carefully found my footing on the ground. Vampire strength or not, no one wants to risk blowing out a knee.

Noise rose from the front of the building as the partygoers spilled into the street. We headed in the opposite direction and emerged on a parallel street to the south. In this area of town, the subway stations were farther away from the water, so we hurried west.

"There!" A sign glowed in the darkness across the street from an Asian pastry shop. "We'll catch a train and be long gone." The scent of pineapple, coconut, and rose swirled around us as we approached.

We were about to cross the street when I heard my name called by a friendly-sounding voice.

James and I froze.

Lily ran out of the pastry shop. "Zelda! What are you doing here?"

I forced a smile and tried not to look back over my shoulder to see if a horde of angry vampires was behind me. "I could ask you the same thing!"

"My friends wanted to go to Lady Wong Pastry & Cake. Not much that's gluten-free there—but we're going to stop by Posh Pop for cupcakes later. I have a dietary restriction," she added, cheerfully, to James.

"Me too," he said.

I stared at him. "You what?"

"I have a dietary restriction."

Lily looked back at me, presumably waiting for an explanation or an introduction, or both.

"Oh! Lily, this is James. He might be helping out at the shop."

"I—what?"

"But we have to get back, so... enjoy the cupcakes! Talk soon!" I waved, then hauled James to the station stairway.

The train slid into the station. The doors opened, and we collapsed into seats. A map of the subway system hung opposite, all red, blue, green, and yellow squiggles across a white background.

"What were you thinking? '*Me, too. I have a dietary restriction.*' Has anyone ever told you you're not good at improvising?"

"That's rich, coming from someone who rang a church bell to announce their escape."

"We got away, didn't we?"

"Yeah. But where am I going to go? They're going to be looking for me now."

"You can sleep anywhere." I elbowed him. "You can hang upside down like a bat."

"Very funny."

In the rattling white noise of the northbound train, we both fell silent.

Too many questions. Too many unknowns.

I leaned my head against the glass and closed my eyes. The map reappeared behind my eyelids—

Except instead of subway lines, there were red, silver, and gold vines traced across a field of green.

17

Carriage lamps glowed on the graceful townhouses. Although many had gone dark inside, there were enough lit windows to spill golden light on the sidewalks. We ascended the stairs to Victorine's townhouse, and I knocked as loudly as I dared.

Claudette yawned as she opened the door. She let us into the entryway and told us to wait.

James thrust his hands into his trench coat pockets and paced.

I hoped he didn't bolt. Not after all that work.

Claudette returned. "Follow me."

We were ushered into a library I had never seen before. Wingback chairs faced a cold fireplace. Built-in bookshelves filled the walls all the way to the ceiling. Almost everything seemed to be fashioned from the same richly polished dark wood, and the air smelled of lemon-scented polish and old paper.

"Wait here."

The door closed with a quiet *click*.

James, who had taken a seat, leaped up and resumed pacing.

"Settle down, man. We're coming to her for *help*. What do you think is going to happen?"

"What do I think is going to happen? Do you even know how any of this works?" He shook his head. "What I did is tantamount to snitching on a mob boss. How do you think Al Capone would handle it?"

The door opened.

Victorine entered. Other than her thick white bathrobe, there was no giveaway that we had banged on her door at a far later hour than would be considered civil.

James bowed.

The vampiress sat in a wingback chair. Recessed spotlights illuminated her hair like a halo. She didn't even glance at me. "James Aurelius Monroe."

He didn't look up. "My Lady—"

"Silence." Her fingers curved over the armrests. "I have every reason to throw you into the street and let the wild dogs finish you off. Betrayal of your Elder carries a sentence of death."

"Please—" He caught himself, closed his mouth. Fell to his knees. His gaze stayed on the floor and sweat glistened at his temples.

"However..." She glanced at me. "There are exceptions."

James didn't move.

"One: In the face of a greater threat to the Blessed, an Initiate may request asylum from another Elder. Two: If the Elder accepts the defection, they accept responsibility for said Initiate as long as they both shall live. James Aurelius Monroe, do you understand me?"

"Yes, Lady."

"By transferring your allegiance you will withhold no secrets, tell no lies, and accept all tasks I may ask of you, disregarding all peril that you may serve as I tell you."

"I will, Lady."

"Look at me."

James raised his head. Every trace of world-weary sarcasm had been washed away.

"I am Victorine Laguerre. I have killed my Elder. Your first Elder died for disobeying the Covenant. The Covenant must be followed above all else. Do you understand?"

"I understand."

She lifted her hands and held them out.

He moved forward and took them, still kneeling. It looked, for a moment, like a marriage proposal.

"I will accept your defection. You will lodge here until I have settled the matter."

"Yes, Lady."

"Be seated."

James swiftly rose and took another chair.

"Zelda, ring the bell."

Her air of authority had me moving automatically—before I checked myself. "I'm not your Initiate. I'm your tenant. You want to boss someone around, find someone less obstinate."

James's eyes widened.

"I'm sure I couldn't find anyone *more* obstinate," she replied.

"Allow me." James jumped to his feet and rang the bell.

"Thank you, James," Victorine said.

In a few moments, a bleary-eyed Claudette appeared.

"Claudette, kindly bring a decaf coffee service. Then return to your rest. I will manage my guests." Victorine did not speak while we waited. Only when Claudette had delivered the coffee and retreated did she continue. "Tell us, James: What were your intentions with Zelda that night?"

James swallowed with some difficulty. "We—that is, Jessica and I—we were told to bring Zelda in. Lord Prospero had some questions for her."

"About?" Her voice was mild, but her expression was altogether harder.

"About the Seal. He wanted to lock the Gentry into their realm," said James. "Forever."

I looked at Victorine. "You wanted me to fix the seal. What's the difference?"

"The difference, my obstinate friend, is that the Seal was designed to last a few decades more. A blink in time, as the Gentry reckon it. It was never intended to be forever."

"Is it... a *nice* place? Where they are?" I tasted the coffee. Pretty good, for decaf. I needed a good house blend for the shop.

Victorine set down her cup. "I have never been there. No one but their kind has. But it is their home, and they went willingly to it. I have heard that it is green and gold, a forest kingdom unspoiled."

The gold vines from the subway map retraced themselves in an intricate pattern in my mind's eye. I glanced at my hands, where the thorny red stems of vampire magic entwined with the lacy silver embers of Poppy's magic. "Everyone wants me to do something with the Seal."

"You are the only one who can."

"I'm guessing it would suit his purposes if the Gentry disappeared forever? Less competition or something?"

"Lord Prospero has greater ambitions than holding court. He wants more. Of what, exactly, I cannot be sure," Victorine said. "But he is a fool if he thinks the Gentry would be his only opposition. The Blessed have survived this long only by forbearing to overstep our domain."

I set down my coffee. "I need to see the Seal. The sooner the better. Where is it?"

Victorine looked to her new Initiate. "James," she said, "you may retire to the red bedroom on the second floor. It is currently unoccupied. I have things to discuss with Zelda."

James stood and bowed. "Of course, Lady." He left the library and closed the door behind him.

"You don't want him to know?"

"The fewer who know any secret, the better. Lord Prospero already knows, certainly; but he may not have told his Initiates."

"So where is it?" I imagined it to be in yet another one of the innumerable rooms in Victorine's townhouse.

"It is in a museum."

"In *public*?"

"Hiding in plain sight."

"Which one? The Met? The Guggenheim?" I ran out of the ones I knew off the top of my head. Then I thought of the one with the funny name: "The Frick?"

"The Mirror Seal hangs in a private room in the New-York Historical Society. I will arrange for you to visit it."

"You said the Seal was originally made with witch magic, right?"

"The Gentry crafted the mirror. The witches designed the spell. The Blessed contributed to the magic. Your grandmother wove everything together."

I nodded. "I want a witch with me."

Victorine considered. "It is not an unreasonable request. Did you have one in mind?"

"I'll bring my roommate, Poppy."

"Can she be trusted?"

"Can anyone?"

"Now is not the time to get philosophical. But if you wish to have her assistance, I will not stand in the way. And now," she said, "go home. You need your rest. You cannot live on borrowed magic alone."

"I can try."

"Even the Blessed must take their ease from time to time. You may suffer exhaustion of the mind, even if your body has boundless energy."

I had the sneaking suspicion that her concern was more like a craftsman's care for his tools, but she was right. "I'll show myself out."

"Until tomorrow, then."

I left the townhouse, then followed the street west to Park Avenue.

Central Park lay on the other side of the avenue. In Grandma's time, no lone woman with sense would have entered the park late at night. In modern times, crime was much lower, but the idea of crossing in the dark still brought my feet to a stop at the crosswalk.

But this wasn't the eighties, and I wasn't a child. I was an adult with magic. I could make myself look like an overgrown bruiser. Blast a few fireballs. Use my Blessed strength to twist an arm or two. If anything, I could be the scariest thing on those trails.

The habit of fear dissolved into a getting-away-with-something delight.

I crossed Park Avenue and entered. I'd have to get across the park before it closed, but as long as I took long strides, I should be through and out in not much time at all.

There were few people on the path. Lamps lit the pathways with circles of light that didn't always join to the next one; there were places where the shadows ruled. As I left Park Avenue behind me, the night sounds rose: a far-off horn, distorted by distance; my own footsteps; a lonely bird call. Instead of fearing a mugger behind every tree, I relaxed into moving freely.

It seemed as if I were underwater rather than on land. The branches waved in the current of a summer breeze. Fields of smooth grass resembled an ocean floor more than plain earth. Even the fallen leaves drifted in a watery way. I half-expected a mermaid to swim out from the depths of the wood. The wood was *alive* in a way it hadn't been during the day.

When at last I reached the other side of the park and exited onto the Central Park West sidewalk, I patted my pockets without thinking. Had I left something important behind me? A wallet? Keys?

Then I realized—it wasn't something tangible.

It was a small piece of my soul, lost to the midnight ramble.

18

On Monday, after an extra-long walk, Poppy and I left the dogs settled into the living room for their customary afternoon snooze. Then we departed on foot for the New-York Historical Society.

"Ooh, I'm so *excited*," said Poppy. "No one's ever invited me to examine an artifact before. I mean, my family owns a few, but I wasn't allowed to touch them. I think they thought I'd break them or something." She laughed. "They were glad to see the back of me."

"When you left for the States, you mean?"

"I can see you picturing me on the Queen Mary or something. It wasn't half a century ago, you know. I flew on an airplane, like a *normal* person. My parents said I could go anywhere I wanted, so long as it wasn't within a thousand miles of them. Mind reading and flame throwing aren't quite the *thing* in their circle."

I laughed in near-disbelief. "What? They sent you away?"

"I'm an embarrassment, apparently." She twirled as she walked. "Poppy, that's terrible."

"No, no, no, it's all quite fine. I *like* New York, really I do. And no one cares who I am or where I come from. Until they find out about the mind reading, of course. What about you, though? I mean, I know some things, but it's more fun if you tell me all the details."

So I told her all about me: my childhood in Florida, summers in New York, restaurants I'd worked at. My shabby but cozy old bungalow in Orlando's Milk District. Adopting Jester. My near and extended family: Mom and Bruce; Aunt Belinda, Luella, and Lily.

"How lovely." Poppy gave a wistful sigh. "I hope I shall get to meet them all."

"Lily's right here, of course, at NYU. And Bruce is in D.C. But the rest of them are pretty firmly rooted in Florida."

We approached the New-York Historical Society, which faced Central Park and stood in the shadow of the more well-known American Museum of Natural History. A knock at the side door brought the sound of steps in heels.

The door opened.

A curator in a tailored black skirt suit and white blouse gestured us in, then led the way without another word. Her neatly pinned hair reflected the hallway spotlights. We followed her, turn after turn, like mice in a maze, until we came to a second door.

She opened the door and stepped back. "You have one hour."

"Thank you," I said.

Poppy dropped a tiny curtsy.

We entered.

The Mirror Seal hung by itself on one of the gray walls. It was a full-length mirror, but larger than average—not just taller, but wider, too. Carved branches, leaves, and flowers adorned the ornate wood frame. Small marble birds nestled in the nooks. Sparkling crystals made it seem as if the whole frame was covered in pinpoint stars. The silvery mirror glass looked like frozen waves—so fogged and distorted I could hardly tell if I was looking at my reflection or something on the other side of the mirror.

Without thinking, I reached for it.

"Wait." Poppy lit a handful of fire and swept it over the surface without making actual contact. Fiery, fractured reflections lit up the glass. "You never know with these old things. It could be booby-trapped."

"How can you tell if it is?"

"You can't, necessarily." Her tongue poked out of her lip as she concentrated. Then she withdrew. "I think it's okay."

"It's not going to explode?"

"Probably not."

I examined the glass more closely. There, along the trough of one of the waves, was a hairline crack. It extended from the top right corner of the mirror to the bottom left, like a wiggly slash. "It's cracked, all right. See this?"

Poppy came closer.

"This is what I'm supposed to fix."

"Oh, I see." She paused. "And how exactly are you going to do that?"

"Good question. Can you lend me your fire magic again?"
She held out her hands.

I took them. Warmth bathed my arms like I'd placed them under a heat lamp. The Mirror Seal reflected the silver fire magic as it crackled over my hands and crawled up my wrists like a traveling flame. It settled into thin, lacelike patterns, as if I'd put on opera-length gloves of silver netting. "Thank you." With Poppy's magic, I could see the silver enchantment woven throughout the mirror. But at the hairline crack, where I expected to see it unraveled, it was intact. I pointed to the crack. "Are you seeing the same thing, here?"

"Hmm... glass is cracked... but the magic is—not," she said.

"If the witch magic isn't broken, what is? The magic of the Blessed, or the Gentry?"

"Must be the Gentry. They're the ones who'd be trying to break free. Right?"

"Right." The Blessed wanted to lock them in, not let them out. "So how do I fix the crack without the Gentry?"

Poppy clapped her hands. "It's a catch-22! You can't fix the crack without the Gentry, but the Gentry are still locked inside."

"Rats." I ran my hands over the frame again. The carved birds were so lifelike they looked like they might startle and take wing at my touch. I felt each detail carefully, hoping to find some clue. "Maybe I can strengthen the other magic to compensate." I would need to come fully empowered with Victorine's magic to try that.

Poppy brought her face close to the mirror's surface. "I wonder what it's like behind there. If it just *shattered*, would they all come galloping through on great big white horses?"

"What makes you think they have horses?"

"They're supposed to be close to nature, aren't they? All that frolicking in the woods and such—well, when they weren't killing the Blessed with beautifully carved handmade stakes."

"I'm sure I'd feel much better about being stabbed if the stake were beautifully carved."

"Would you?"

"No."

"I mean, I like being a witch," Poppy said, "but the Blessed and the Gentry have *style*."

"Witches have style, don't they?"

She regarded herself in the fogged mirror. "Look at me. I'm a trainwreck of boringness. Where's my high-collared cape? My mouse-skin slippers? My cobweb coronet?"

I made a face. "Mouse-skin slippers?"

"You know what I mean."

I stood next to her so that we both fit into the distorted reflection. "I'm not sure I do. I've been wearing the same denim and black combination for decades because it works."

"Don't you have any *romance* in your soul?"

"Poppy, the only romance in my soul is for good food and my dog."

"You're impossible. What about the ex-boyfriend who sent you that honking big knife?"

"Daniel?" I laughed. "That's not romance. That's mutual fascination bookended by dangerous levels of hormones."

"That'd do for me," Poppy said. "You know, when you think of him, he has this really *smolder-y* look—"

I cleared my throat.

"Back to business. Right you are."

I moved closer to the mirror. Raised my right hand, rested it on the wooden frame. My eyes closed. I gently ran my fingers over the warm wood and the cool marble birds. My thumb grazed a dewdrop crystal. For something meant to serve as a seal, it had been made with a surprising amount of beauty and care.

"Is that your gran?" Poppy said.

My eyes flew open. "What?"

"The mirror—when you were touching it, I saw a woman who looked like you. Tall, broad-shouldered. Same eyes."

I peered at the wavy reflection of my face. "But I wasn't picturing her at all..." I tentatively put my hand back on the frame.

"There she is again!"

This time, I kept my hand in place.

Poppy closed her eyes. "I see her. She's at the mirror with a bunch of other people. They're taking her hands. One of them is a woman, very fancy, with white hair. Something's happening—oh!—it's like your magic, Zelda. And now she's facing the mirror alone. There are strings of magic; it's like she's braiding them up together and they're sinking into the mirror. The mirror is shining all over, different colors: red, silver, gold. Quite pretty really. And now... oh, now it's gone."

Red, silver, gold. The Blessed, the witches, the Gentry. The magic should have been all I could think about. Instead, I saw a different braid: a sweet braided bread filled with cinnamon, apples, butter, and sugar. How Grandma cleared a counter to lay out the dough. How she helped me add the filling down the middle. How her hands guided mine to braid the strips together. How she steadied the knife to cut slices when it finally cooled.

Ingredients. Instructions.

A recipe.

Now I just had to find one for mixing three magics.

19

After examining the Mirror Seal, I hustled to the restaurant. Daniel was coming, and I wanted to make sure everything was looking at least halfway to gorgeous. I certainly wasn't going to leave Berron to do it without me.

The glass door swung open with its familiar bells, and Berron popped up from behind the glass case. "You're in earlier than I thought you'd be."

I grabbed a smock and tied it on. "Is that bad?"

"Not at all. In fact, it worked out for the best. Here," he said, handing me an insulated paper cup.

"What's this?" I sniffed. "Oh! Coffee. Perfect."

He picked up a second cup. "You told me you were looking for a good house blend for the shop, so I've been taste-testing my way through the Upper West Side."

"I had you down as more of a cappuccino guy."

"Nah. Good coffee is good coffee, no matter how you take it." He leaned against the counter. "This cup—this cup right here—is unlike any other that ever has been or will be. How much sunlight touched the leaves? How much rain fell? What breeze shook this plant that didn't shake the one down the hillside? All those conditions are gone. They'll never be exactly the same again. Drinking coffee is like tasting time itself."

I peered into the cup. Berron had a weird way of looking at things, but he wasn't wrong. I'd often thought the same thing about summer fruits like tomatoes and strawberries. "Drinkable time, huh? But how does it taste?"

"Let's find out." He held his cup aloft. "To coffee."

"To coffee." Maybe it was his words playing tricks on my mind, but when I drank it I could taste cool mountain air, soft clean rain, even humble dirt. It was mellow and rich and rolled gently over the tongue.

A spark of profound satisfaction lit his eyes, and for several moments too long, I couldn't look away. They were mesmerizing. True mahogany fringed with black lashes.

My cheeks felt warm. Too much hot coffee at one go. I put the cup aside and got to work, fixing and scrubbing and polishing until I heard the bells jangle once again.

Someone had entered the shop.

I wiped my forehead and glanced up from where I'd been attacking a stubborn stain on the tile.

I saw the shoes first: shaped and polished leather providing a landing for the hem of tailored pants. The sweep of fabric upward to a belted waist. Pearly buttons north to a crisp collar. Stubbled jawline.

"Daniel!" I clambered up from the floor and threw my sweaty arms around him. "Thank you so much for the knife. It's gorgeous."

He returned the hug, and his spicy cologne momentarily blotted out the shop's scent of dust and cleaner. "You're not still mad at me?"

"Of course I'm still mad at you. That way, you'll have to keep making it up to me." I released him and faced Berron. "Berron, this is Daniel, my—friend. Daniel, Berron is from Columbia. He's part of a program that's helping me restore the shop."

Berron held out his hand. "Any friend of Zelda's is a friend of mine."

Daniel returned the handshake with what looked like slightly more force than necessary. "Likewise."

Like a lightning flash, the sun bounced off a passing car and flickered over the two of them. Standing there, face to face, they were like dueling sculptures. Daniel, solid and polished, composed, at ease in the world and confident of his power in it. Berron, tall and graceful, gently scruffy, comfortable with hard work yet philosophical about coffee beans.

Berron picked up his coffee and took a sip. His gaze rested steadily on Daniel. "Did you come here to help?" he asked, with polite-sounding curiosity.

Daniel, who was rarely caught off-guard by anything, hardly hesitated. "I would be glad to help."

"You're not really dressed for it, though," I said.

"Sure I am." He unbuttoned his cuffs and began rolling his sleeves, eyeing Berron the whole time.

"Don't you have to go to work?" I asked.

"I'll be late." He loosened his tie, pulled it off, then draped it around my neck. "Here. Looks better on you than it does on me."

I laughed and snapped it at him like a whip.

Berron set down his coffee and flexed his hands. "Why don't we start by getting that broken equipment out to the street?"

"Let's do it," Daniel said.

While the gentlemen wrestled refrigerators to the curb, I busied myself with the glass display case. I wasn't going to let it be hauled away, not yet, not before I'd at least made an attempt to salvage it. I'd fixed things before by taking them apart, cleaning them up, and putting them back together. If I got lucky, Grandma's vintage case would carry on its proud role in the newly opened shop.

I couldn't help looking up every now and again as they passed by. Even the way they carried a heavy load was different. Daniel carried weight like a longtime gym member: with strength, concentration, and control. Berron, on the other hand, lifted like a ballerina's partner—you never saw the effort.

I hadn't meant to rope Daniel in at all, but I could have guessed that Daniel wouldn't turn down a challenge, even if it was delivered as inadvertently as Berron's innocent question.

I peeked out from behind the glass case. Now they were outside, laughing it up over something. Daniel was punching Berron in the arm in a friendly way. Berron faked a wrestling move where he threw a knee to Daniel's chest.

They were coming back. I withdrew behind the case again.

Their energy filled the shop as clearly as the sound of the bells when they came through the door.

"You didn't tell me this guy made custom furniture," Daniel said.

"It's just a hobby, really—"

"Look at this." Daniel took out his phone. "These are from the workshop he moonlights for." He displayed a website with pictures of tables made with rich, glossy wood in a variety of colors and grains.

Berron shrugged, with an almost guilty look.

"You've got to make me a coffee table," Daniel added as he scrolled through more pictures.

"He's making me a bar," I said. "And tabletops."

"Wow, Zelda, how do you *get* so lucky? You got a four-leaf clover tattooed somewhere I haven't seen?"

Somewhere he hadn't seen? Oh, now he was trying to push Berron's buttons. Not with my imaginary tattoo as a prop, he wouldn't. "No. But maybe I'll get one. Where should I put it, Berron?"

Berron spoke to me but aimed a lazy smile at Daniel first. "I think your shoulder would be an excellent canvas."

Why was my weird brain generating a startlingly vivid image of Berron tracing the art onto my skin? I shook my head and took a deep breath.

"I should be going," Daniel said.

"Wait—" I hurried behind the counter and retrieved the gift box. "I promised I'd try it out for you. Only..." I looked around for something to cut.

Berron rummaged in his bag. "How about this?" He held out a small, shiny green apple with blushing patches of pink.

I took the apple and cupped it in my hand. It was barely larger than a golf ball. "It's perfect. And so small! Where did you get this?"

"I picked it last night."

"You *picked* it?"

Daniel, out of Berron's line of sight, rolled his eyes.

"Found an old tree growing wild in Riverside Park. Not far from where we were the other day, actually. I'll take you there sometime, if you like."

Daniel removed the lid of the box, took out the knife, and laid it on the counter. "Let's see what this will do, shall we?"

I reached for the knife, then drew back. "Let me find something to put under it."

"Oh, that reminds me." Berron reopened his bag and pulled out a wooden cutting board with contrasting stripes of wood. "I threw this together. Thought you might like it."

Daniel's ears turned a shade of pink that matched the apple.

"I love it!" Then I winked at Daniel. "Let's try them both out." With the apple, the knife, and the board rinsed and dried, I took the knife in hand. One smooth slice removed one curved side—the knife was as sharp as it looked. Laying the apple on the newly flat side presented another curved side. A cut, a turn, another cut and a turn, and I had all four sides of the apple. After setting the core aside, it was quick work to cut each piece into even slices.

Daniel and Berron went quiet as they stood and watched.

"See?" I said, holding out the board with a neat array of apple slices. "The knife and the cutting board work together. The board provides a stable landing that won't dull the blade." I set down the board, plucked two slices, and playfully presented one to each of them. "Enjoy the fruits of your labors. I certainly do." With that, I grabbed a slice for myself and crunched down.

They bit into their slices, and the scent of apple swirled between us.

Sweet.

Tart.

Wild.

Nothing had ever tasted this good.

20

Poppy galloped out of the kitchen as soon as I came home. Georgiana trotted happily beside her. "Zelda! We have a guest!"

I dropped my bag, then quickly scooped it back up before Jester decided to use it as a chew toy. "A guest?" Down the hall, I spied a swirl of black followed by a leaping Jester.

The swirl of black belonged to a long black coat. "Can someone contain this poodle, please?" said James.

I hurried to the kitchen as he dodged Jester's enthusiastic jumps. Jester seemed to think it was a grand game. "Jester, off. Jester, sit. Jester! Sorry about this," I added to James. "He's a nut." I grabbed the dog mid-leap and scooped him into my arms. "What are you doing here? Is it—*safe* for you to be out?"

James pushed his dark sunglasses back and grinned. "*Safe* is overrated."

"Is that so?" Poppy tilted her head. "Then why are you imagining being stabbed to death by a bunch of people wearing black?"

His mouth fell open.

I shot her a look. "Poppy!"

"Sorry! Would you like some tea, James?"

"Tea?"

"Yes, tea. Lovely stuff. You drink it?" She mimed the action with her little finger sticking out.

"She reads minds," I said to James.

He edged toward the hall. "I should go."

"No, please, do stay," said Poppy. "I'll concentrate on the dogs. They don't mind." She gave Georgiana an affectionate pat. "Isn't that right, darling?"

James tucked his sunglasses into an inside pocket, and gave a philosophical shrug. "It's here or Victorine's."

The three of us slid into seats.

"You're not actually roaming the streets," I said.

"I am not. She has placed me under her protection, but I don't have the freedom of the city."

"So why are you here?"

"Why not?" His boyish grin was charming, but had a certain fatigue behind it.

"You don't have anywhere else to go, do you?" said Poppy.

James and I looked at her.

"What? I don't have to read your mind to pick that up. Besides, I understand perfectly."

"You do?" said James.

"Of course. You've lost your little pack."

"We're not werewolves."

"The Blessed might as well be, the way you stick together even when you have literally nothing else in common."

He raised his eyebrows. "You are... not wrong." He laughed, and for the first time, it was an easy, unrehearsed sound. "How do you know all this stuff?"

Poppy set her cup down with a decisive *clink*. "You don't get to midlife as a mind reader without learning a few things."

"I'm as old as you are, thank you very much," James said.

Poppy stared at him.

James shifted uncomfortably. "What?"

"I see it now," she said. "What you look like. What you *really* look like, that is."

Jester laid his head on James's knee.

James looked down. "Oh—hi, dog."

"You can pet him, you know. He doesn't bite," I said. "Well, not people, anyway. He's pretty fond of biting everything else."

He hesitated, then petted Jester's fluffy head. "I had a dog."

"Was he a very good boy?"

"They all are," Poppy said.

"Girl, actually. Used to sit on my foot to make sure I couldn't go anywhere without her."

Poppy and I *aww*-ed in unison.

He gave Jester a scratch on the chin. "Sometimes I still feel it. A warm weight on my foot, when I least expect it."

Poppy patted his arm. "Come on. Let's do something fun."

"No, really, I shouldn't have barged in on you—"

"Nonsense. Zelda, wasn't I just saying that it would be fun to go to that charity auction today?"

"What?"

She widened her eyes at me.

"Oh, *that* charity auction! Right. Yes."

"We'll need help carrying our packages home," added Poppy. "And it's neutral territory—open to everyone, even the Blessed. In fact, your new patron helps with it. She runs magical fundraisers along with the mundane ones."

Georgiana, also looking for pats, nudged her head under James's other hand.

"And we could bring the dogs!" Poppy beamed.

I looked at her. "To a fancy charity event? Are you sure dogs are allowed—"

Poppy landed an elbow in my side.

James was too occupied with petting Jester and Georgiana to notice. "Yeah, okay. I'll go."

"Splendid!" Poppy winked broadly at me.

Outside, Poppy and Georgiana took the lead. I fell back with Jester to walk beside James. "How do you wear that thing?" I said, nodding at his long black coat. "It's boiling."

James glanced down. "This? I've always worn it."

"Have you tried wearing something that doesn't look like it came out of a nineties time capsule?"

"Why bother? I don't fit in anyway. Might as well wear what looks good. Good sun protection, too." He lowered his shades briefly and looked me up and down. "You don't exactly 'dress your age,' either."

He had me there. "All right. So if we were to dress like grownups, what would we wear?"

"If I tried to dress my age, I'd look like a kid in his dad's clothing." He nodded toward Poppy. "Your friend has it down. She makes it look good."

"Poppy?" She was currently half-skipping, half-walking next to Georgiana, like she didn't have a care in the world.

"She's lucky."

I thought about what Poppy had told me about her family, and had to bite my tongue to keep from outright contradicting him. "Some people would think you were lucky."

"More like cursed." He shoved his hands in his pockets.

Poppy paused to let us catch up, and Jester surged forward. "Have you been before?" she asked.

James shook his head. "I don't think it was Lord Prospero's scene."

"Oh, it's marvelous," Poppy said. "All kinds of lovely things."

A triple set of iron gates marked the entrance to the building. Each pair of gates stood between tall, round columns. One pair opened beneath a deep red canopy with the address painted in neat gold script. Instead of coming right up to the street, like most buildings, this one had its own plaza inside the gates, with wrought iron tables and chairs with red cushions that matched the canopy. The front of the stone building curved in a concave half-moon shape, and a second floor echoed it with a smaller but similar curve.

As we passed through the open gate, I noticed the letters L, W, W, in a fancy entwined font, emblazoned like a seal on the wrought iron. "What's LWW?"

"League of Women's Welfare," Poppy called over her shoulder.

"Ladies Who Witch," James murmured.

As Poppy approached the doorman, her spine straightened, and her chin lifted. Even the hand holding Georgiana's leash took on an imperious air. "Poppy Spencer-Churchill."

The doorman checked a list on his clipboard. "Welcome, Miss Spencer-Churchill." He eyed James and me like we were last week's fish.

"And these are my guests," said Poppy without missing a beat.

Georgiana sat, with her tongue lolling, as Jester investigated the doorman's shoes.

The doorman opened his mouth as if he might say something, then closed it.

Poppy marched on. "Come along!"

We followed.

The entryway doors opened to a large ballroom with a swooping double staircase leading up to a second-floor gallery. Gleaming white marble with black veins covered the walls and floor and surrounded a fireplace so large a cab could have parked in it without a scratch. On the ground floor, fashionably dressed women surrounded white-skirted tables and filled the air with a hum of talk and laughter.

"I feel underdressed," James said.

"You feel underdressed? At least you have a jacket." I doubled my grip on Jester's leash. I didn't need him to go hallooing off after someone's designer bag dangled too low.

"Oh, *hello*, Mrs. Winchester!" Polly said with a wave. "Don't worry," she added quietly, "they get all sorts in here."

James raised his sunglasses. "I feel much better now, don't you, Zelda?"

In addition to tables filled with a fancy buffet of fruit, cheese, meat, and desserts, there were even more tables of merchandise. I spotted a table full of orchids, and a familiar face behind the flowers. "There's Victorine." I pulled Jester away from where he was attempting to bite the edge of a table skirt and headed for the orchids.

Victorine eyed us coolly as we approached. "I did not expect you here."

"Poppy brought us."

Poppy gave a cheerful wave. "Hello! Lovely orchids."

James looked slightly ill. "Lady Victorine."

"And you brought your dogs." She leaned forward to get a better look at Jester. "It is said that the word puppy comes from the French *poupée*, or doll. Hello, *poupée*."

Jester cocked his head and looked vaguely confused.

"We're going to, uh, shop around." I let Jester pull me away. Besides Victorine's orchids, there were so many things to look at.

A nearby table held glass snow globes—except, on closer inspection, they weren't just snow. One contained a tiny desert complete with a miniature cactus and a skull. A tiny sandstorm billowed inside. Another globe held dark water with little gray clouds swirling above.

Poppy held one up. "I like this one." The globe held beach sand and oh-so-small waves crashing on the shore.

I smiled. "Reminds me of Sparkle Beach."

The next table held a collection of papers, greeting cards, envelopes. Another witch stood behind the table, this one with a fitted purple velvet jacket over a t-shirt that read, "We Didn't Start the Fire. Oh Wait—We Did."

"Fire witch humor," Poppy said. She picked up a box of paper. "Ooh, self-igniting. For all your *spicy* correspondence."

James had wandered over to another table. Like Victorine's, this one also held plants—but all different varieties. The witch at the table adjusted her large cat's-eye glasses and held a potted flower plant up for inspection. "Everything is earth witch grown—we have organic chamomile and borage, rosemary and rue... are you looking for anything in particular?"

"Just browsing," said James.

We were moving on when a blur of motion caught my eye, followed immediately by a crash.

Jester was nose-deep in a pile of dirt, broken clay, and something green.

"Jester!" I dove and scooped him up. His face had that mulish look he got when he wasn't about to let something go. Leaves, stems, and roots stuck out of his jaws. "Drop it!" I grabbed some of the green stuff and pulled. "What is this stuff? Is it poisonous?"

Poppy handed Georgiana's leash to James.

"What am I supposed to do with this—"

"Shut up, James," said Poppy. "Now," she cooed to Jester, "open your jaws and let Poppy have the nice plant."

Jester tightened his bite.

"Listen, you little maniac," I said. "You're going to let this go, right now, or you're going to get a *big time-out*. You hear me?"

The earth witch came around the table. "That is my prize good luck clover and it's *very* valuable."

I rolled my eyes. "Whatever, lady—is it *poisonous*? Poppy, look it up."

"Right!" She whipped out her phone.

I looked around. "Where'd James go?"

James came running with Georgiana loping alongside at full speed. "Here." He held out a translucent slice of expensive-looking ham.

Jester looked torn. His jaws worked as he debated whether to drop the green stuff or see if he could manage to grab the ham while also keeping the green stuff in his face.

I took the ham and waved it in front of Jester's nose. "Drop it, and you get the yummy ham."

Jester's jaw opened and closed, opened and closed. Finally, a wad of mashed green clover hit the floor with a wet *slap*.

"It's not poisonous!" Poppy cried triumphantly.

Jester happily gulped the ham.

The earth witch crossed her arms. "Yes, well, it's still very expensive."

"I'm so sorry." I pulled out my wallet. "What do I owe you?"

She told me.

The marble floor dropped out from under me.

I emptied my wallet. Poppy and James emptied theirs, too. My cheeks burned. "I'll pay you back."

Poppy waved her hand. "Nonsense."

"You have to admit—this dog knows how to party," James said.

I handed over our cash.

And I thought that was the most excitement we'd have at the charity auction.

21

The hum in the room faded with a hiss like someone had thrown water on a fire. There, at the head of a group of newcomers, stood Jessica. Jet-black beads sparkled from ropes of necklaces layered over a black crop top and a long black skirt with a thigh-high slit. She strode into the room, high heels clacking on the marble floor, sweeping the crowd with her deeply shadowed gaze. Then she stepped aside. "My Lord."

James swore, quietly, and spun away from the direction of the door. Georgiana let out a quiet growl, and Poppy gripped the leash tighter. Jester wiggled in my arms, either trying to run away or to burrow himself into my shoulder.

A male voice cut through the silence. "Thank you, my dear Jessica, but I believe we require no great fanfare here. We are here to shop, are we not?" From within the group, a man emerged. His figure, while not tall, was compact, well-formed, dressed in an impeccable if somewhat old-fashioned suit. His hair curled with brown and gray strands, slightly messy, and a thick but trimmed beard outlined his jaw beneath gold-rimmed glasses. With unlined skin and youthful

175

bearing, his age could have been anywhere between thirty-five and fifty.

He stopped, cane in hand, one leg casually bent as if posing for an old-timey photo. "I would enjoy supporting a charity. How very novel. We lack novelty, these days." He looked like nothing more than a young college professor.

Until his gaze went to me, and it was red.

"I should so enjoy a new amusement," he finished.

With that, his entourage fanned out to the tables.

Prospero. Or *Lord* Prospero, as he styled himself. The witches at the tables eyed each other but remained at their posts while the Blessed moved through the room.

"We should go. Now," said James.

"I'm not leaving. He doesn't scare me."

"Yeah, well. He should."

"Go stand behind Victorine if you need to. I'm not going any-where."

James took a step toward the orchid table, then pivoted and came back. "If you're going to stand here like an idiot, then so can I."

I glanced at my roommate. "Poppy? You want to get out of here?"

"Pshaw." Poppy tossed her hair back. "I'm not scared of some el-der Blessed with a whole army of underlings and a really frightening way of crashing a party." She edged slightly behind James. "Well, maybe a *little* bit scared. But not a lot!"

Prospero took his time crossing the floor. Although he put no weight on the cane, it clicked the marble with each step.

I wasn't sure whether I'd look tougher with Jester in my arms, or on the floor. Neither one was a good option, but you don't want your poodle trying to lick your enemy when you're having a serious chat. It doesn't give the right impression.

So I kept holding him.

Though conversation still murmured, I could feel attention shifting to the two of us as Prospero approached, like we were magnets and everyone else was iron.

"Zelda Hawkins. You are a difficult woman to track down."

"To kidnap, maybe."

"Kidnap?" His eyebrows rose, almost comically, above his fine gold-rimmed glasses. "That's a bit harsh, wouldn't you say?" His gaze shifted to my new vampire friend. "James? Cat got your tongue?"

James looked like it was taking all of his willpower to stay in one spot, let alone answer his former master.

He looked at Poppy. "And who's this pretty lass?"

"I'm Poppy Spencer-Churchill to you, you—*awful man.*"

Prospero chuckled. "Such a charming group, aren't you? And dogs, too. Are they your mascots?"

"What do you want?" It was really, *really* hard to sound intimidating while Jester licked my ear.

"I would like for you to do me a small favor."

"From what I heard, it's not small. And I have no reason to do you any favors."

He rested both hands on the cane. "Don't you? Has my colleague already bought you off? Do you belong to *her*, now?" He nodded toward the orchid table.

"I don't *belong* to anyone." I didn't add: *except this dog*.

"You may not find her to be the benevolent mistress you imagine. I, on the other hand, can offer you what would exceed even your wildest dreams."

"Is that why James was so glad to get away from you?"

Prospero's eyes narrowed with a flash of rage that was gone, smoothed over, almost before I could be sure I'd seen it.

Almost.

He took one step closer and spoke in a quiet, even tone, for my ears only. "In the end, I will get what I want. You have only to choose whether it is *with* you—or *through* you."

The scent of candied violets wafted from behind me. "Lord Prospero."

Prospero stepped back. "Lady Victorine."

"Have you come to acquire new goods?"

"Indeed. There is one item in particular that attracts my interest."

"Ah, but what if you cannot afford it?"

His gaze locked on mine. "I pay in currency no one can refuse."

"Strong words, Lord."

"Actions, Lady, will prove them out. Good day to you." He turned, unhurried, and made his way toward the exit. His entourage filtered out of the crowd like a school of fish, then followed him out.

They were gone from sight before I realized my stomach was doing flips and my heart was pounding. I buried my nose in the fur on Jester's neck and breathed. "It's okay. The nasty man is gone."

"Are you talking to your dog, or yourself?" said James.

"I didn't see you smarting off in front of Prospero."

"Quiet, James." James paled. Victorine turned her calm gaze to me. "What did he want?"

"To hire me." I set Jester down. "I guess he doesn't realize I'm self-employed. A small business owner. Part of the backbone of America. Just because I take a side gig"—I acknowledged Victorine with a nod—"doesn't mean I'll work for anyone who asks."

"You go, girl," Poppy said.

"And now, I'm going home. I have a menu to finish writing. This restaurant isn't going to open itself."

"James, you will accompany them."

"Yes, Lady."

I shook my head. "That's not necessary—"

"Furthermore, you will stay there until further notice. I am not leaving you two to your own devices. James will stand guard."

I looked at Poppy. She shrugged. "Fine," I said. "But it's *temporary*."

We left Victorine behind and made our way toward home, skirting the southern edge of Central Park before heading north.

"What was it you called that place, James?"

"The Ladies Who Witch."

Poppy slapped his arm. "You're not supposed to call it that. It's the *League of Women's Welfare*."

"Same thing, isn't it? A bunch of rich women who get together to eat hors d'oeuvres and raise money for charity. Only these happen to be elemental witches."

"I wonder if they need a caterer," I said.

James scoffed. "Only you would walk out of a tug-of-war between two Elders with a new and improved business plan."

"Witches need to eat, too."

"Speaking of which—oh, I made a pun! Get it?" said Poppy. "Anyway, I'm absolutely *starving*."

"Come on. You two can help me in the test kitchen."

Jester, who had very food-specific word recognition, perked up his ears and licked his chops.

Back in the kitchen, I tied on an apron and retrieved Grandma's menu in its plastic sleeve. "One of the big things on these old menus is Virginia ham. See?" I pointed to the menu. "Dry-cured. Slow-smoked. Aged. People always think that quality ingredients are some kind of new invention, but they're really not. Everybody likes a quality ingredient. Your grandparents did as much as we do today." I hauled a stack of ham slices out of the fridge. "Second, you cannot underestimate the importance of a good Cheddar. Vintage menus had plain Cheddar cheese sandwiches. Just cheese!" I pulled out a variety of Cheddar cheeses. "So we'll start with the basics. The foundation. We're going to pick a Virginia ham. We're going to pick a Cheddar. Make sure they play well together. You ready?"

James looked dubious.

Jester took a flying leap at the counter.

I moved the food out of range and began cutting it into samples. I was already picturing the glass display case with one of everything on display, each on its own individual wooden cutting board, a treat for the eye. I passed the samples to Poppy and James.

"I don't usually eat..." he said.

"Taste the damn ham, James."

He chewed and swallowed dutifully.

"Poppy?"

"I quite like this one. Bit salty, though. I'd give it—a *seven* on the scale of one to ten hams."

"James?"

"Reminds me of bag lunches. In a good way."

I smiled. "Nostalgia is a trap for the appetite."

We nibbled our way through the rest of the samples, laughing and joking, tossing cheese bits to the dogs, until the sun set completely. James said goodnight and withdrew to the couch. Poppy and I and the dogs headed upstairs.

Before she entered her room, Poppy turned back. "Zelda?"

"Hm?"

"Can I talk to you for a moment?"

I opened my door and we both went inside. At night, the midnight blue walls played tricks on the eyes—if you squinted, the walls might not be there at all.

"You know I try not to concentrate on what other people are thinking, right?"

I nodded.

Her gaze went to the floor, and her usually sunny expression faded. "Sometimes it's hard not to see. That man—the Blessed—"

"Prospero."

She shuddered. "I can't—"

I took her hands, squeezed them. Her fire magic silently entwined our hands with tracings of silver embers. "It's okay. You can tell me."

Her gaze lifted to mine, and her eyes looked haunted. "Even as he's chatting with you and saying everything so calmly, he's"—she squeezed her eyes closed—"he's picturing these terrible things—"

"Hush." I hugged her. "I'm so sorry. You should never have to see anything like that."

"I don't mean to, you know. I can't help it. I hate it. I wish it would go away."

"I know." I patted her back.

"Just—be careful."

I let her go. "I hate to ask you this, but what about Victorine?"

Poppy dabbed at her eyes with her sleeves. "Yes. She's... different. Most people are so scattered, their thoughts flip from one image to another like clicking a View Master as fast as you can. But she's laser-focused—all of her concentration sits there like there's nothing else in the whole world beyond what she's looking at right then."

"She is intense. And... James?"

Poppy laughed weakly. "He's fine. He thinks about having a lawn *a lot.*"

I laughed, too. "Well, that's a relief."

Both of us reached down to pat the dogs. Georgiana and Jester accepted the affection with sweet doggy smiles and unbelievably strong cheese breath. Not for the first time, I envied their simple existence. I didn't need to get showered with treats for looking cute, but there were days when navigating the realm of humans and paranormals sounded far less appealing than a life of walks, naps, and the occasional stolen mouthful of clover.

22

We were so close to finishing the shop that when I woke up too early the next morning, I couldn't bear to stay in bed and try to fall back asleep. I rolled over to a view of thick gray clouds boiling in the sky. I got dressed, walked Jester, set out his food and water. Then I bent low to snuggle him and scratch his cheeks the way he liked best.

He'd gotten something glittery in his fur.

"What have you been into, boy? The craft supplies?" I didn't have any, but I wouldn't have put it past Poppy to be into that sort of thing. Whatever it was, it was extremely sticky. I tried to brush it off as I headed for the parlor. No luck. Tiny pinpricks of shine covered my hands.

James was on the couch, staring out the window.

"James," I said quietly, not wanting to wake Poppy and Georgiana. "Top me up, will you?"

He held up his hand like he was waiting for a high-five.

I clasped it, inhaled, felt the burning magic of the Blessed sink beneath my skin. Strength and speed, energy and rushing blood.

There were advantages to having a vampire in the house. "Thanks, man."

"Anytime."

Outside, the air smelled of water and ozone. Thunder rumbled in the distance. I hurried to reach the shop before the sky decided to fall. Berron wouldn't be there for another hour, most likely, but I could keep going from where we'd left off.

The bodega lights were on, so I stopped there first for a cup of coffee. Inside, the resident cat paced restlessly on top of an ice cream freezer. He paused, flattened his ears, and yowled unhappily.

"What's up with him?" I asked.

"He's been doing that all morning. Probably the storm."

"Animals are weird like that."

"You're telling me."

I carried the hot paper cup out. Raindrops hit the sidewalk with a slow, uneven tempo; bullets in slow motion. I unlocked the door and entered.

The first thing that hit me was the smell—sharp vinegar and garlic—before I even registered the shattered glass, the liquid, the pickles themselves, all over the floor.

The coffee slipped from my hand, struck the ground with a *pop*. Scalding liquid bathed my legs, but I couldn't make a sound.

Every table and chair had been overturned. Several were missing legs.

All the dishes I'd collected covered the floor in pieces like it was Saturday night at a Greek restaurant.

My carefully organized binders had been opened, crushed, and their contents scattered.

Impact dents and deep scars covered the newly installed wood bar.

Half the reach-in doors were torn off.

The tiles I'd carefully scrubbed and repaired crunched underfoot where they'd been smashed.

Even the back room hadn't escaped—the panel had been torn off the new refrigerator, and handfuls of wires spilled out.

I walked behind the counter. There were shreds of old paper piled neatly on the untouched wooden cutting board, arranged like someone wanted me to find it, to inspect the pieces of paper, to hold them in my hands and turn them over one by one until I understood the meaning.

West.

Side.

Sand. Crossed out with a red pen.

Wiches.

A cry erupted from my gut.

I had to breathe. Breathe. Grip the edge of the countertop to hold myself up. Breathe some more.

They destroyed my Grandma's restaurant. My family's restaurant. *My* restaurant.

I pay in currency no one can refuse.

I smashed my hand onto the counter.

Then I heard the jingle of bells.

Berron backed through the door with an armload of boxes. "Hey, Zelda, I brought the—" He turned. His face fell as he registered the devastation. "What the—" He set down the boxes. He touched the fallen chairs. The overturned tables. His graceful hands traced the wounds on the bar.

I wanted to speak. Wanted to say something. But if I opened my mouth, I was going to cry.

Berron picked up a chair missing two of its legs. I could hear him breathe. His hands tightened—then, with no warning, the chair was flying across the room. It hit the wall with a crash that rattled the broken crockery.

The shock drained my tears away. I stared at him. "What the *hell*, Berron? Isn't it already bad enough?"

He turned. The look on his face was enough to make me take a step back. "I'll kill them."

"You don't even know who—"

"I can *smell* them."

"You *what*?"

He wasn't listening. Instead, he pawed through the mess, trying to set anything right. "Rotten, soulless degenerates. Think they can do whatever they want. Think they own this city."

"You going to sniff them out like Sherlock Holmes? I didn't think that was in your skill set." I watched him pace through the mess. "This is *my* restaurant, remember? I want these criminals caught, too."

"Criminals. Yes. They're rotten, soulless, degenerate criminals." Every word spat in time with another movement to pick something up. "And I'm going to put them all in the ground."

"What are you going to do, hit them with your graduate degree?"

He straightened. "That's low."

I came around the counter. Standing before him, he seemed taller and broader than I remember. His easy strength suddenly seemed bent on an entirely different purpose, one I hadn't seen before. I knew him as a builder, a creator.

Now he looked like a god of destruction.

But I hadn't spent years in male-dominated workplaces filled with wannabe-machos and the occasional ex-criminal just to get bowled over by a sudden display of rage. "Stop having a fit. I have to fix this. Can you get some more help from your department, maybe?"

"My department?" He looked lost.

"Okay, okay, fine. I'll get my friends. Maybe they can pitch in, help us get back on track."

"You mean Daniel?"

"Yes, Daniel."

He frowned.

"Don't make that face. I don't know what your deal with him is, but he's nice."

"He's acceptable."

"I didn't ask your opinion. Plus there's my roommate, and my brother if I can get him to haul his butt up here." I thought of James. "And another friend of mine."

"Zelda."

"What?"

"Why would someone do this to you?"

I looked away. "Random crime. It's a big city."

"You don't have any enemies?"

I forced a laugh. "I'm a middle-aged sandwich chef. My only enemies are over-zealous restaurant inspectors and the New York City Department of Buildings. Neither of whom are into trashing restaurants." I hazarded eye contact with Berron.

As our eyes met, I felt the truth come crawling up my tongue. That I had pissed off a powerful vampire. That he was going to try to scare me into doing what he wanted. That I didn't know what he would do next. That for the first time in my life I was truly afraid.

I blinked.

There was a moment of lost time, like when you're driving and you don't remember the journey between point A and point B. Nausea gripped my belly, and the room began to tilt.

"Whoa, there." He swept off his knit hat and placed it behind my head, cradling it as he helped me sink to the floor. He was almost fastidious in his touch, taking no liberties, his skin never whispering next to mine, only with layers of fabric between us.

"I'm sorry—"

"Hush, now. What have you eaten today?"

"Coffee."

"Here." He offered another small apple from his bag. "I washed it."

I took it but didn't bite. "You're doing so much for me, and you don't even ask for anything in return. Where did you come from, Berron?"

He smoothed my hair back where it was falling into my face. "Manhattan, born and raised."

"Florida's not like this. It's a lot quieter."

"I'd like to go there someday."

"You've never been?"

He shook his head.

"Maybe when you finish your program."

He smiled, softly. "Maybe."

I closed my eyes, leaned my head back. I could spend all day cleaning up the mess. But what would stop Prospero and his goons from wrecking it all over again? He wasn't going to stop until he had what I wanted, or I gave up and left.

All I had to do was walk over a bridge and I'd be beyond his reach. But if I did that, I'd be walking away from everything I came here for.

A new start.

My own business.

The embrace of magic, learned those long-ago summers with Grandma.

It wasn't just walking away from what I came for. It was walking away from what was rightfully mine.

"Give me a trash bag."

"You're in no state—"

I pushed myself up. "I'll get it myself." I bit into the apple, letting the sugary juice rush over my tongue. I finished it in a few bites, whipped open a trash bag, and threw in the core.

"Police? Insurance?"

"They'll just slow me down." I didn't add that the last thing I needed was to draw attention to myself. "And this *looks* awful, but most of it can be put right with sweat. I don't mind a few scratches on the bar. Gives it character."

"You're the boss."

"Damn right, I am." I grinned and tossed Berron the box of trash bags. "I'll be telling this story over this very bar, just you wait."

And I almost, *almost* believed it...

Until I spotted a white envelope nestled inside the broken glass case.

While Berron's back was turned, I retrieved it. The envelope was inscribed with my name in the thick cursive swirls of an old-fashioned fountain pen and sealed with a dollop of red wax. I unsealed it.

Dear Friend,

I find myself with a great desire to continue our conversation. Although your friend Daniel's company is most enjoyable, I fear he is too fatigued for further conversation. Kindly grant me the favor of your unaccompanied presence without delay.

Yours, etc.,

Lord Prospero

I had just enough time to read an address before the entire letter flashed into ash and collapsed.

He had Daniel.

I whispered a curse.

"Did you say something?" Berron looked over his shoulder. "You want some more to eat? That apple couldn't have been enough. What sounds good?"

I hid my ash-smudged hands behind my back. "I—uh—I can't. I just remembered I have to do something. It can't wait."

"I'll come with you."

I pictured Berron, wide-eyed, exposed to the world of magic. Another outsider forever looking in. Look where that had ended up. "I got this."

He looked like he wanted to argue.

Could he sense my unease? "Please," I said. "Don't worry."

His hands went to the scarred wood. "I'll be here. I'll keep worrying—I mean, working."

I nodded and left.

Rain drenched me in seconds. Where were the cabs?

I ran to the nearest cross-street. The next cab sped past, drenching me in gutter water. I lurched toward another one and watched it take off at top speed. The next cab coming up the street didn't look like it was about to stop, but I threw my hand up anyway.

With a screech of brakes and a spray of water, it stopped. I threw open the door and jumped in. "Gramercy Park."

23

The cab pulled up before an old multistory red brick building fronted with double columns, and windows that would have been at home in an old Gothic cathedral. I paid the driver, hopped out, and hurried to the oversized wooden doors.

Unaccompanied, he'd said.

I had arrived in Manhattan that way, if you didn't count a miniature poodle. But since then a constellation of people had gathered around me: Lily. Victorine. Berron. Poppy. James. Even if I could have brought help without endangering Daniel even more, how could I put any of them in harm's way for a mistake I had made? I'd gone to Daniel. I'd led danger to his door. That meant it was my responsibility to lead that danger away. To negotiate. To bluff. To do whatever was necessary.

Alone.

The entrance was unlocked. Inside, the faint sunlight that had managed to sneak through the rain was muted even more by stained glass windows and the dark wood paneling that absorbed their light.

I found the elevator tucked into a corner. I pressed the button, and when the doors slid open, I stepped inside. Though many New York elevators were small, this one seemed designed to squeeze the air out of you.

As the tiny elevator crawled upward, I examined my hands. The tracings of fire magic and vampire magic were still strong. Although I'd been at a disadvantage with James and Jessica before, even vampires would hesitate in the face of a fireball. I might not be able to kill a vampire that way—but I could make them regret living.

The seventh floor arrived with a jolt. I lit small fires in my palms and entered a narrow hallway with dim yellow lighting. The shadowy corridor dead-ended at a door with gold apartment numbers above.

The door whipped open before I could knock, and Jessica stood before me. Her dark lipstick looked worn away in the center of her lips, as if she'd rubbed them with a napkin. "He's waiting for you." She smirked as she stepped aside to let me pass.

Fire played over my fingers.

The entryway rounded a corner to a parlor with satin-upholstered chairs, ornate wallpaper, and side tables draped with miniature tablecloths. Old portraits hung above the fireplace mantel. It was not entirely unlike Victorine's hidden library, but this room appeared to have gone without updates for at least a century.

"Ah, Miss Hawkins." Prospero entered the parlor, cane in hand, as casual as you please. "Do I have the honorific correct? You are never married?" Before I could speak, he continued. "Forgive me for the personal question. I have a terrible weakness, you see. My curiosity."

"Where's Daniel?"

"Patience, my friend."

"I'm not your friend. And patience is not a virtue of mine."

He chuckled. "Nor mine, I confess."

"If this is some kind of ruse—"

"I assure you it is not. No more so than the alterations to your place of business."

"Did you think that would get me to do what you wanted? Wrecking my place?"

His eyes assessed me. "I was afraid it might not. Thus I arranged to leave the letter which so conveniently brought you here. I appreciate your timeliness, by the way."

I couldn't help looking all around the room, as if I would spot Daniel behind a piece of furniture, like a high-stakes game of hide-and-seek. "Stop stalling, Prospero, or I'll burn this place down around your ears."

"No, you won't. You wouldn't endanger the rest of the building." He leaned on the mantelpiece. "I fail to see why you have cultivated such animosity toward me. I only wish to have the rights and freedoms that you take for granted."

I had to resist the urge to shut him up by flinging the nearest tchotchkes at him. "Let me guess. Those 'rights' and 'freedoms' have some mysterious link to the Mirror Seal becoming permanent."

"Exactly so."

"Well, I don't negotiate with terrorists."

Prospero's smile was thin. "How original. But before you label me, ask yourself: What is it *I* want that is so different from what *you* want?"

A laugh escaped me. "You're kidding, right?"

"Come to the window."

I watched every step as I moved closer.

"Do you see the park below?"

"Gramercy Park. So?" I hated being lectured on a *good* day. This was not a good day. But I suspected that interrupting would drag this out even more, so I let him talk.

"One of only two private parks in all of New York City. Only the surrounding residents are allowed to have keys. Lose a key, and it will cost you one thousand dollars. Lose it again, and you will pay two thousand. Imagine how special residents must feel when they enter this coveted place."

I peered down at a round planter in the center of the park. A ring of flowers surrounded a statue of a man. Leafy tree canopies rose around it like tethered hot air balloons. Even in the rain, it could have been beautiful—if I were in the mood for pretty scenery.

"Now imagine the gates close behind you. They lock. You rattle the iron bars to no avail. You are trapped. Not for an hour, not for a day. *Forever*. How does that park look to you now? Like a paradise? Or a prison?" He gazed at me. "Your new friend, James. Did you know that his family moved away when he was young?"

"I don't see what this has to do with—"

"How will he see them if he is trapped on this island?"

"They can come and visit him."

"They have full and busy lives, and little desire to travel. To James, they might as well have moved to the moon. He will rarely see them again, if ever."

I scoffed. "If you care so much about James, why is he terrified of you?"

"Great generals are rarely understood by the rank and file."

"What's to understand? You want to trap the Gentry in their own prison. *Forever.*"

He tapped his cane smartly on the floor. "Theirs is not a prison. It is a wondrous land—the stuff of dreams; of poems; of song!"

"Some would say the same about Manhattan."

He shook his head. "Loosed upon the world, they will hunt us all. Our only chance is to escape—now, before the One Hundred Year Peace is up, or they find some devious way to break free."

"I have a funny feeling they'd say the same thing about you."

Prospero regarded me steadily. "You will not help me."

"I will not lock up the Gentry forever just because it suits your purposes."

The tick of the clock spat into the silence.

"Jessica," he called, "bring in Miss Hawkins's property."

Another door opened into the parlor. Jessica staggered through, sideways, as if hauling a heavy weight.

Then I saw the arm around her shoulder. A drooping head.

And the expensive clothing of a man I knew all too well.

"Daniel!" I reached for him right as her careless grip would have dumped him on the floor. I caught him just in time and guided him down to one of the satin couches. "Oh, my God. Daniel!" I cupped his face. "What did you do to him?"

But even as I said it, I saw it.

Two marks on the side of his neck, leaking blood. Tiny dots of red on his fine shirt.

"He's dying," Jessica said, with the air of someone being helpful. "I got him close. But not all the way, if you know what I mean." She laughed.

I had never killed anything in my life. Yet at that moment, I knew: I was going to kill *her*.

But I couldn't do it then—I had to save Daniel.

My hand went to his pulse point. His pulse was there—faint, but there.

"He's too far gone," added Prospero, carelessly. "No one can save him now."

Basic kitchen first aid: apply pressure to the cut. I snatched the tablecloth from the nearest side table, sending knick-knacks crashing to the floor, and pressed it to the wound. "You did this before I could even answer you! Even if I'd have said yes, he'd still be dying!"

"Ah, but that's the way the game is played, Miss Hawkins. It's played to *win*. And now you know the consequences for losing. Come, Jessica," he said, offering his arm. "We will take a walk in the park." He dangled a shiny, sturdy key from a chain, then swiftly pocketed it.

"You can't leave him to die! Fix this!"

"If it weren't for you, he wouldn't be here in the first place. Consider that when placing the blame. Good day to you, Miss Hawkins. After you bid farewell to your friend, kindly shut the door on your way out. We will clean up the... *mess* when we return."

They sauntered out.

"Daniel, please—wake up—" His skin looked the wrong color. I didn't have much time.

What was I going to do?

With my enhanced strength, I could carry him out. But by the time I got him downstairs and into a cab, it would be too late. Same for trying to get an ambulance here.

But how could I sit helplessly and watch his life ebb away?

Prospero was right. It was my fault. If I hadn't gone up to his condo that afternoon, flirted with him until he let me stay, this wouldn't have happened.

That night when James and Jessica broke in, we'd playacted as vampire and willing victim. Even if they hadn't found *me*—if they'd found "Victorine"—I had made Daniel look like someone of importance. It had put him on their radar.

I thought I'd saved us.

I'd doomed him.

But maybe...

I pulled out my phone, my hands shaking, and called James. "Pick up, damn it."

"Yeah."

"James! I need your help."

"No one even calls each other anymore, Zelda. Can't you send a text like a normal person?"

"James. Shut up. I know we're not supposed to talk about anything over the phone, but I am about to break every rule in the book, so just listen, and whatever you do, *don't hang up*. Are you there?"

"Yes…"

"Okay." I took a deep breath. "I need to know how to convert someone."

Silence.

"James?"

"You can't be serious—"

"Daniel is going to die if I don't. Prospero and Jessica could be back any minute, and I don't have time to argue, just *tell me what to do*!"

"I don't even know if you *can* do it—"

"I have to try, for God's sake." My voice broke. "*Please*."

He didn't have to say a word for me to hear every misgiving that flitted through his head. If it worked, he'd be cursing someone else to the hellish existence he longed to escape—and my own life would be forfeit for breaking the Covenant of the Blessed.

After an eternal pause, he spoke. "You have to bite a good artery."

"There's already a mark—will that work?" I switched the phone to speaker mode and set it down.

"Yes. You'll have to bite down and… ingest… while activating your magic. I've never done it, I've only had it done *to* me, but I know you have to mix your own magic with the essence of the victim—and then return it to them."

"Right." I stared down at Daniel, utterly horrified by the idea of what I was about to attempt, but concentrating on growing out my fangs at the same time, just as I had done at the Arcade to nick my own finger. "Talk me through it, okay? It helps if I hear a friendly voice. Say whatever." My unnatural strength came in handy as I raised Daniel's upper body so I could get behind him. I couldn't shake the eerie, guilt-ridden feeling of having done it all before.

Daniel's skin felt too cold. I tried to be gentle, moving his head to the side, but it fell with a sickening lack of resistance. I lowered my lips over the cuts, and for a moment, I thought I would throw up—but I punched the arm of the couch as hard as I could and let the pain knock me back into control. "Hang on, Daniel. I've got you."

I bit down and blood flowed. I tried to put my mind somewhere, anywhere else, but the sensation—as visceral as carving a roast—dragged me right back to exactly what I was doing. I summoned the magic, let it burn through me, up my hands, my arms, my neck, numbing and igniting my lips at the same time.

James was talking, talking, and I let it wash over me, a soothing radio broadcast on the edge of sleep.

I had to let the magic in.

Except it wasn't just the magic I was letting in. It was Daniel. Not only the physical, although the iron taste of blood wouldn't let me forget that for a second, but the soul of Daniel himself. I was a goddess of death and rebirth, remaking him in an image of my own creation.

Whatever we had been to each other in the past—friends, lovers, exes—this would change everything. He would be one of the Blessed: strong, fast, a lifespan far beyond human.

He would not die.

He would heal.

He would live.

And if he cursed me for it after, I would understand.

24

Daniel gasped. His back arched. His chest expanded as breath rushed into him. His eyelids fluttered before he relaxed into my grasp again. Warmth once again radiated from his skin, and his heartbeat drummed into a regular rhythm.

Only then did I become consciously aware of James's voice. "Zelda? Are you there? Did you do it?"

I lifted my head. Pressed my hand to Daniel's forehead, smoothed away the sweat. "I think so."

"You have to get out of there."

"He's still unconscious." James was right, though. I couldn't predict what Prospero and Jessica would do if they came back. Or what a fight could do to Daniel's precarious condition. "I—I'll have to carry him."

"Just get him downstairs and into a cab. Take him to Lady Victorine's. She'll know what to do."

"What if she kills me on the spot for breaking the Covenant?"

"She won't kill *him*. They didn't kill me when I was converted, remember? Just my Elder. And technically, you're not one of the Blessed. Maybe that will save you."

"Oh, that's reassuring."

"Get off the phone and go."

I hung up. Rather than risk waiting for a cab to drive by, I ordered a rideshare, then put the phone back in my pocket. I maneuvered Daniel into a fireman's carry and stood. Although I had plenty of strength, each step took extra care not to whack him into a wall or doorway.

If Prospero and Jessica returned, I would blast them—very carefully—with fireballs, until I could get past with Daniel.

And if other building residents saw a middle-aged woman carrying a grown man down the hallway, well... this was New York. Stranger things had been seen.

I managed to open the door and enter the hallway having only bumped Daniel's head once or twice.

The count went up to three as I squeezed into the world's tiniest elevator.

I stumbled slightly as I exited into the lobby. Balancing Daniel on my shoulder, I checked my phone and saw the car icon indicating my ride pulling up in front of the building. I took the steps down to the sidewalk and out to the street. I opened the door and managed to tip Daniel into the backseat.

I hopped up front. "Too much to drink," I said.

The driver shrugged and pulled into traffic. "Bottled water?"

"Yes, please." I usually said no, but this time I greedily drank the room-temperature water, cleansing my mouth of blood before discreetly checking my appearance in the flip-down mirror. My lips were redder than usual, and my cheeks flushed, but other than that there were no signs of what I had done.

The driver pulled up at Victorine's townhouse in minutes, and I wrestled Daniel out. With considerably more difficulty than I had put him in.

Claudette opened the door, but Victorine was right behind her, heels clicking in rapid time on the marble floor.

She fixed me with a glare so fierce my stomach curled up and tried to wrap around my spine. "What did you do?"

"Can I please come in? I think this might attract a little more attention than you're used to."

She huffed and stepped aside. "Take him to the red bedroom."

I carried him upstairs and tipped him gently onto the bed. Like me, he was flushed.

Victorine approached. "You converted him."

"I had to."

She gripped his wrist. Felt his neck. "This has never been done before. There is no precedent."

"Does that mean you won't kill me for breaking the Covenant?"

"Your victim may decide that."

"*What?*"

"Not only did you convert someone during the Peace, but you converted him without his consent. He did not ask for this."

"He was going to *die*."

"There are worse things. Ask James."

"What was I supposed to do, exactly?"

Her gaze softened. She stroked Daniel's cheek. "We all play God from time to time. Your grandmother would have done the same."

"My grandmother wouldn't have gotten into this mess in the first place." We stood side by side, watching him. His state had eased into something more like sleep. Already, he looked indefinably more youthful. "I know this probably isn't the right time—"

"I'm sure it isn't."

"... but I am absolutely starving."

"It is not unusual after a conversion. Go down to the kitchen and help yourself. I will stay with him."

The kitchen was impressively equipped but looked hardly used. An unused kitchen has an air to it, a loneliness, that sets it apart from a kitchen that's just very clean. The interior of the refrigerator was carefully arranged and untouched. I had to assume Victorine stocked food for the staff and none for herself. It wouldn't raise too much alarm for a wealthy woman of the Upper East Side to barely eat; trim figures were a blood sport around here.

I rummaged around and decided on a simple ploughman's lunch: bread, butter, cheese, pickles, some ham, a sliced apple. Could have used a good cider to go with it, but you can't have everything.

I assembled the spread on a board and seated myself at the acre-wide kitchen island just as I heard a new voice from down the hall.

"Oh, good Lord! Where *is* she?" Footsteps came in my direction. "Zelda?"

Poppy entered the kitchen.

I stopped with a wedge of double Gloucester halfway to my mouth. "Poppy? What are you doing here?"

"James told me."

"Oh." I couldn't think of anything intelligent to say after that.

"Right," Poppy said, briskly. She poked at my lunch. "What have you got here?"

"It's a ploughman's lunch."

"Bah. If you're going to do British food, at least do something good. Like a curry." She wrinkled her nose and continued to poke at the items on the board. "What is this? I mean, it's not a sandwich, it's not a cheese toastie, it's just—"

"Can I eat it? Do you mind?"

"Sorry." Poppy seated herself at the island.

"Where is James, anyway?"

"He got sent on some kind of errand."

I took bites of the bread, cheese, and pickles. Though my palate recognized the food as tasty, delicious even, and my stomach rumbled happily, on another level it was like eating wood chips. Like I had split into two people: old Zelda, who liked to eat, and new Zelda, who didn't deserve pleasure of any kind.

What had I been thinking, moving to New York? Abandoning the life I had in Florida for a mad quest to restore—what? A restaurant in a city full of restaurants?

And taking a magical side gig on top of it? Who did I think I was?

Not my grandmother, that's for sure.

My stomach turned, and I pushed away the board.

"Can I try that, then?" said Poppy.

I slid it across the island.

I was a royal screwup. I didn't deserve to be here. I didn't belong in this town, not on any level. I was a tourist. It had been the height of arrogance to think otherwise.

Poppy made happy noises over the ploughman's lunch. "This is pretty good, actually."

"I'm glad you like it." Except *glad* seemed as far away as home. I squeezed my eyes shut, rubbed them with my fingers. Home wasn't even a sanctuary; what would I say to Mom? To Bruce?

"Are you all right?" Poppy said.

"Yeah." I lowered my hands and forced a smile. "Yeah, I'm fine."

"You don't *look* fine. Also, I'm trying not to see the pictures in your head right now, but... they're pretty strong."

"What do you see?"

"You *want* me to see?"

"Nothing could possibly get any worse."

Her look of concentration shouldn't have been charming, but it was. "I see a small wooden house with a sagging front porch. There are bushes outside with big pink flowers. A rusty red hatchback in a dirt driveway. Short, stubby-looking palm trees."

"Palmettos. They're called palmettos."

"Palmettos, then. Is that your house?"

"It was. Before I gave it up and moved here."

"It's funny, with your ability to copy magic, that you don't get my ability to see things like this."

"It's hit or miss. Like with the Blessed. I get the strength, the healing, the senses, the"—I swallowed, remembering my teeth on Daniel's neck—"the ability to convert someone. But not the extended life."

"Are you going to go home?"

A laugh came out that had no humor in it. "Home? I was only renting that house. I sold that car in Jersey. I quit my job. I told everyone I was going to make it in New York. I don't even know where home is, anymore."

"Maybe you do."

"Spare me the inspirational talk." I felt like a jerk even as the words left my lips.

Poppy stared down at a broken piece of bread. "Maybe home isn't a place. Maybe it's something you carry inside yourself. Knowing who loves you; who cares for you. And it doesn't matter where they are, or where you are. You're always home when your heart is open to them."

My throat tightened. As much as my Mom and I disagreed on my career path, as much as Bruce acted like an ass, they cared for me. I cared for them. It didn't matter that we were scattered across the eastern seaboard. And whatever this strange group that had formed around me turned out to be—Poppy, Victorine, James, Berron, even

Daniel, if he didn't hate me after this—there was something of home, here, too.

Claudette entered the kitchen. "Miss Laguerre asked me to tell you: He's waking up."

Part of me wanted to crawl into a kitchen cabinet. But the braver part of me stood up and climbed the stairs to the red bedroom.

Victorine still stood in attendance next to the bed. When I approached, she stepped aside.

Daniel turned his gaze to me.

Red. Just like the other Blessed.

If I thought my throat was tight before, it tightened further as I tried not to cry. "Daniel."

"Hey, Zelda." He sounded like he'd been sick with the flu.

"I'm so sorry, Daniel." I went to my knees beside the bed, laid my hands on his, lowered my forehead to the crisp sheets. His new magic began to wrap around my fingers.

I could have made excuses. I could have begged forgiveness. But at that moment, I couldn't do anything but kneel, with my head laid on the bed, and wait to be judged.

He placed one hand on my head, stroked my hair. Vampire magic tickled my scalp. "You always were a bad habit."

"Daniel..."

He hushed me. "Victorine told me the basics."

I raised my head, looked questioningly at her.

"We have never had a conversion like this," she said. "However, we will have to assume, until proven otherwise, that he is one of us. That he has the magic of the Blessed."

It felt traitorous to hope Daniel didn't hate me. I deserved his anger. I deserved to be told how I'd ruined his life.

"I'm not on the outside anymore, Zelda."

And with those words, the balance between us suddenly changed. Before, I'd held the upper hand. I was the flirt, the charmer, the one with the fantastic secret. Despite his own formidable charm, his incredible wealth, Daniel had always been one step behind, one rung below, always chasing, always reaching for that part of me he couldn't have for himself: my magic.

It didn't matter how weak he looked. He knew, and I knew, that we had just become equals.

You think that's when everything settles.

It's not.

It's when even the tiniest movement makes the ground shift under your feet.

25

I needed to think, and moping around Victorine's wasn't going to do the trick. Neither was curling up in bed and hiding from the world. I needed to put my hands on something real.

Returning to West Side Sandwiches was as close as I could get to going home.

I expected to find Berron still at the restaurant, but he was gone. No note. Maybe he had stepped out for lunch. I didn't own his time—everything he did was basically a colossal favor—but being around someone who *didn't* know I'd just turned my ex-boyfriend into a vampire would have been comforting. Uncomplicated. I needed more uncomplicated in my life.

He'd been busy in my absence. All of the debris had been picked up. The reach-in doors reinstalled. The tables and chairs had been righted, although the wooden table surfaces still had dents.

Strangely, though, the wood bar looked like it had never been damaged. Dozens of marks had disappeared like magic.

I ran my fingers over the wood, feeling for divots. None. It was as smooth as it had been the day it was installed. Had he somehow polished it down? There *was* a smell of wood in the air, but it was more the scent of sap than sawdust.

I grabbed a rag and a bottle of window cleaner and attacked the front window. Blue liquid spritzed, then ran down the window as I scrubbed and wiped years of dust and grime. Slowly, the street outside came into focus—people and cars in full technicolor rather than a browned-out blur. I dug my rag-covered fingertips into the sill, the edges, and the corners, unwilling to let even a speck of dirt hide. I tossed the filthy rag aside and took another, then repeated the process. I did another two rounds with the glass in the front door. By the time I was done, my muscles had begun to twinge with the effort.

The afternoon light glowed through the clean windows. Finally, I could see clearly.

I set down the bottle and took a seat on a barstool. My hands lay on the wooden bar. Silver magic and red magic sparkled from my fingertips to my elbows. On top of that, whatever glitter had gotten on Jester was still clinging to my skin.

I flexed my fingers. Grandma had combined different magics to enchant the Mirror Seal. I would have to do the same to repair it. But how?

Maybe I could practice. A mirror was nothing more than an ordinary object until it was filled with magic. Could I do the same to something else?

I got up, moved behind the counter and picked up the chef's knife Daniel had given me.

Only one way to find out.

I washed my hands, then laid the knife on Berron's cutting board and placed my fingertips on the flat of the blade. Instead of letting the magic in, I had to push the magic *out*.

First, the silvery fire magic. It was like coaxing Jester into a crate when he was too little to ride in the car without one. He didn't exactly want to go in there, but he wouldn't fuss too much once you actually got him inside.

My eyes closed, and my awareness narrowed to the blade alone. Something in the material vibrated in a kind of familiarity—a knowing—

This knife already knew the touch of fire.

Of course. Worked metal remembers the flame of the forge.

I'd found my way in.

Tiny silver flames bubbled on the surface of the blade, not burning, not melting, but becoming part of the structure of the knife itself, a *new* knife—of metal and fire.

But how would I add the magic of the Blessed?

I had a queasy suspicion I knew exactly how to do it. Uncountable kitchen nicks had already taught me: Kitchen knives know the taste of blood.

"Don't be squeamish," I said to myself. There in the quiet of the empty restaurant, it could have been my Grandma talking. I placed the tip of the knife against the pad of the middle finger of my left hand. Easier than nicking it on a tooth, no doubt, but no less painful.

I watched, almost detached, as the sting concentrated itself in one spot and blood welled around the tip of the blade. I gently smeared it down the flat, and pushed the magic to follow it. Red vampire magic wrapped around the metal like barbed wire.

The knife held a story, now—Daniel's, Berron's, and mine. It was Daniel's gift; Berron's apple was the first thing it ever cut; and it was my magic that filled it, my hand that wielded it. The red and silver flickering against each other gave me a glimmer of hope. It also made me want to keep the knife closer.

I wasn't a weapons-carrying kind of person—at least, I hadn't been—but the run-in with Prospero ignited a new desire to never be empty-handed. New York City frowned on carrying knives, though. Unless they were clearly for professional use.

Like a chef's knife.

In a plain kitchen scabbard.

I brandished the knife. "You need a sheath," I said. A call to a nearby kitchen supply store confirmed they had what I needed. One fast shopping trip later, I had the item in my hand. The sturdy leather sheath even had a belt loop for convenient carrying. I paid and headed back to the shop.

I was so eager to get inside and try the knife in the sheath I almost missed that someone was already there. I backtracked from the window, then peeked in. I'd cleaned the glass so well that it might as well not have been there.

Berron.

I heaved a sigh of relief. Of course it was Berron. He'd been out; he'd come back. No ravening pack of vampires had returned to trash the place.

Except—

What was he doing?

His hands were on the surface of one of the wood-topped tables. His head was bowed. His eyes closed. He slid his fingers over the surface, the movement unbroken, a swirl of graceful touch.

The *wood*. The still-damaged tables. The unmarked surface of the bar.

Berron wasn't refinishing them.

He was healing them.

Memories fluttered down like birds returning to roost. That day I felt woozy, when he had never allowed his skin to graze mine for more than a second. The bodega cat that bit, didn't bite him. Jester, who went limp with happiness at one touch of his hand. All that talk of trees and time and restoration—and how he had *raged* at the destruction of the restaurant. As if he could smell who was behind it. Pure fury.

No wonder. His mortal enemy had crashed the place he'd practically adopted.

How could I have been so *stupid*?

I ran for the door and whipped it open.

Berron jumped at the jangle of the bells. Put his hands behind his back like he'd been caught in the cookie jar.

And the table itself? Those dents? Those marks?

Gone. Not by sandpaper, or power tools, or anything in a carpenter's toolbox.

By *magic*.

The door swung shut behind me. I tossed the bag containing the sheath aside, freeing my hands. "Hello, Berron."

"Hey, Zelda, I was just—"

"Take my hand."

He laughed nervously. "What?"

I was stalking him now. "I need to see your hand for a second. You don't mind, do you?"

He tried another laugh. "Is this some kind of new work requirement?"

I was almost there. I lunged for his hand.

He dodged. The movement sent him crashing into the bar.

"Something wrong, *Berron*?" I blocked the path to the door. "Is that even your real name?"

He scoffed. "What are you talking about? You're the maniac chasing me around trying to hold my hand."

"Sure. You're just a regular guy with an unusual relationship to wooden tabletops. Right? Prove it. Take my hand."

"I'm not doing that." His gaze darted like he was looking for a way out. Then he bolted for the back.

I ran.

He hit the back alley door, rebounded. It was locked.

And I had the key.

In the close space of the back room, he had nowhere to go. He turned. His back pressed against the locked door. His hands were hidden behind his back.

But I didn't need hands. That was just one way. "All this time," I said. My voice was low, in control, the purr of a predator cat. "What was the game? Who are you?" I stepped so close I could feel his body heat.

He closed his eyes, a man waiting for the bullet to finish him off.

I rose on the balls of my feet to close the slight difference in height. I was tall, but he was even taller.

My lips touched his. My hands went to his face, cradling it—and a different, golden magic began to spiral down my wrists like leafy vines. Green and gold and darkness and light spun between us in soft whispers, a symphony of sweet meadows and rain, old forests and new, growth and decay, the spinning seasons in all their glory.

"You're Gentry," I breathed.

His lips parted, and he let out a soft noise, like a gasp that hitched in his throat.

And in that reeling moment, he pushed past me and was gone out the front before I could put my feet in motion. I stumbled toward the door, then back, scooping up the sheath. I secured the knife and tucked the sheath in my back pocket. The handle poked my back, but I didn't have time for a better solution.

There are times when you doubt your own conclusions.

Not this time.

If Berron was one of the Gentry, there was only one place he would run.

To where he had come from.

To the broken Mirror Seal.

26

I ran outside as Berron climbed into a cab further up the street.

I waved down a cab of my own, dove in, and told the cabbie to follow Berron's cab. I was about to pull out my phone when a flash of red appeared in my peripheral vision.

Blessed Red.

I turned. There he was—a vampire, on my street, watching me. Watching as Berron and I organized our own yellow cab parade through the Upper West Side. He cast aside a lit cigarette and broke into a run.

"Damn it!" I was being watched, probably followed, and dollars to doughnuts said this vampire wasn't loyal to Victorine. I called James as the cab lurched into motion. "James?"

A pause. "Please tell me you're not about to do it again—"

"Shut up and listen. Get yourself and Victorine to the Mirror." I paused, looking out the back window. "And James? Be prepared. I don't think we'll be the only ones there. One of your 'colleagues' was watching the shop."

"Oh, good. You know how I love a party."

I hung up. Normal life slid by outside the cab, and I couldn't help but feel like I was saying goodbye to it for the last time. I'd made a good run at being ordinary. Apparently, *ordinary* fit me like a pair of too-small kitchen clogs.

Time to embrace the weird.

"Adios, normal life," I said, waving at the world in general. "It was fun while it lasted."

The cab driver looked in the rearview window and raised an eyebrow.

At the New-York Historical Society, Berron leaped out and ran for the main entrance. How would he get to the Mirror? It wasn't like an admission ticket would get you into the back rooms. For that matter, how would I get to the Mirror? The curator had let Poppy and I pass before. Surely I could get in that way.

I paid the driver and hurried inside.

Berron was nowhere to be seen, despite the fact that a line snaked through the lobby from the door to the front desk. Every second that passed was another second Berron was alone with the Mirror, doing God knows what, and I had to get to him before something happened or the Blessed caught up with him.

Whose side was I on, anyway?

My instincts howled to run past the desk, boots pounding the marble floor. Chase Berron down. Demand answers. Yet every guard in the place would have tackled me in seconds if I'd tried. I had to take my place in line like everyone else, like a civilized person, fidgeting the entire time as if I could will it to move faster.

Finally, I got to the desk. My turn to speak.

Was the same curator on duty?

She was not, the attendant said. She was out. At lunch. A fundraiser luncheon, to be exact.

I stared. *At lunch* while the Gentry and the Blessed prowled the corridors. *At lunch* while I stood there, paralyzed, unsure of what to do.

Until I suddenly wasn't.

I smiled. Paid for a ticket. And asked for directions to the nearest restroom. I bolted past a display of antique model ships and took a hard right into the restroom. Inside, I locked the door to the only stall with its own mirror.

Better than Superman's phone booth.

The magic mask on my face lit up at my touch. Every time I used it, it seemed to respond faster, light up brighter, surge with a kind of eagerness that made goosebumps rise on my skin in its wake. I pictured the curator, with her neat black skirt suit and pinned-up hairdo, and diamond glitter cascaded over me, leaving behind its now-familiar aura.

The curator stared back at me in the mirror. There was no time to admire the transformation. I hurried back into the museum hallway, found a door marked "Staff Only," and slid through to the familiar darkened corridors where Poppy and I had been.

A few twists and turns later I was standing outside the room that held the Mirror Seal. Since I no longer needed the curator's appearance, I reverted to my own. The aura of disguise around me faded.

Then I heard the *rat-a-tat-tat* of running feet.

James exploded into view from around the corner, his black jacket billowing behind him.

Jessica rounded the same corner, and with an inhuman leap she threw herself across his back. James staggered and slammed into the wall before her weight finally tipped them to the floor. They rolled like an underwater alligator, all ferocity and muscle, cursing at each other.

Prospero stepped into view at one end of the hallway.

Victorine appeared at the other end. "Go to the Mirror, Zelda," she said, so calm she might have been ordering coffee from Claudette. "James and I will handle our guests."

Prospero raised his cane like a fencing sword.

Before the mayhem caught me, I opened the door and stepped inside.

Across the room, the Mirror hung as before. Only this time, Berron stood beside it. His fingers traced the carved wooden apples and the tiny marble birds.

"Get away from it."

He straightened, but kept his hand on the frame. "Why?"

"I have to fix it and you're in the way." My hand went around my back to unbutton the catch on the knife holster. I drew the knife—Daniel's knife, I'd never think of it any other way—and leveled it at Berron. "Back up."

His smile was sad. "I want to fix it, too."

"Why should I believe a word you say? How much of it was lies? How many times did you put a spell on me?"

"It's dying."

The knife wobbled. "What's dying?"

He nodded toward the Mirror.

"So? The Seal fails. You all escape. Hooray for the Gentry."

Berron shook his head. "Not the Seal. What's inside. Our home. The Fortress of Apples."

The name brought back the taste of the wild apple we'd shared. And the one he'd given me on the day the restaurant was trashed. "Your home is *dying*?" I'd pegged him for being old money, that first day we'd met. But there was something else. Something hiding in plain sight all along. "Who are you?" I said. "Tell me the truth."

He raised his hand, and gossamer gold strands circled him like the paths of orbiting satellites. When they faded, it was like scales had fallen from my eyes, and I saw clearly for the very first time.

He was still Berron—still tall; still with messy, longish dark hair; those mahogany irises—but his posture became straighter and his clothing had changed from beige-and-denim Columbia grad student to a Robin Hood-like outfit of deep green and brown, edged with gold. To top it all off, a gold crown shone on his dark locks.

When, in a sheepish movement, he resettled his hair behind his ears—I saw.

His ears were pointed.

He removed his glasses and chuckled softly. "I always forget about these." He tossed them aside. They skittered across the slick floor. "Whatever else I said, my name is real. I am Berron, the Prince of the Gentry, and I am the only one of my kind to escape this prison."

The door banged open.

Prospero dragged Victorine through, one arm around her neck, the point of his cane pressed to the soft flesh beneath her ribcage. "How convenient. We're all here."

I swung the knife to point at Prospero. "Let her go—"

"If you wish to see this one die before your eyes, keep talking. And you," he added to Berron, "that goes for you as well."

"What do I care if the Blessed murder one another?"

"Go ahead, Prospero," Victorine said, her voice weakened by the arm around her neck, but still proud. "I am prepared to die. My death was foretold by the Arcade."

"Your *death* was the price?" I said.

"What price? What are you talking about?" Prospero's gaze darted from Berron to me. "Never mind. Close the Seal, Miss Hawkins. Make it permanent. We will deal with this stray later."

Berron started toward Prospero. "I'll kill you—"

"No!" I threw out an arm and he stopped. "*Nobody dies.*" I edged backward, closer and closer to the Mirror. "I've had enough of that for one day." As I kept everyone's attention I was pushing my awareness into the knife once again, just like I had in the restaurant.

The golden magic of the Gentry pulsed in my fingers. All I had to do was give it a way in.

And then, I found it.

The knife handle remembered its roots in the forest. Gold vines grew from my hand to the knife, caressing it, wrapping it, and finally sinking into the surface.

Red, silver, and gold magic. And, finally, Jester's glitter... that wasn't glitter at all. It was pure luck, from a mouthful of stolen clover, that had become as much a part of him as his soft, floppy ears and his poofy tail.

I had all the magic, like Grandma, only a little something more. She had been right to create the Mirror Seal. But honoring those who came before you means living in the spirit of their actions, not copying them blindly.

My mom was right. I had to be open to new things.

I knew what I had to do—and somewhere within myself, I could hear her say: *It's the right choice, Zelda girl.*

I smiled at Prospero. "I am going to give you a word of advice, my friend. Are you ready?"

His eyes narrowed.

"Run."

Grandma had always encouraged me to let the magic in. So I did. With a smooth, kitchen-practiced swipe of the knife, I cut the weave of magic holding the Seal closed. The silver and gold magics split with a metallic *twang* and spun apart like cut yarn. To my surprise, the red magic already hung slack, as if it had been tugged loose, but the knife sliced through it just the same, severing it completely. The threads of magic blew outward from the mirror as if they were ribbons on an electric fan.

Prospero's mouth opened in shock. As his restraining arm went slack, Victorine spun expertly out of his grasp, taking his cane with her as she did.

She stepped back to join me. "I think you'd better heed her advice."

Prospero came back to himself. "The Gentry will kill you, too, Lady Victorine."

Victorine held Prospero's gaze and wordlessly held out the cane to Berron.

Berron took it, flipped it, grinned. "Maybe. But not before I get *you* first." He stomped his foot.

Prospero flinched, then flung himself at the door, opened it, and ran.

The door swung shut behind him.

Victorine, Berron, and I eyed each other. Three points of a triangle.

Berron tossed the cane aside. It fell with a clatter. He knelt before me and took my free hand, the one not holding the enchanted knife. He cupped it reverently between his own hands, the same hands that had rebuilt the restaurant from scratch, now the hands that sent tendrils of Gentry magic around my fingers. "Thank you. I must leave now, but I promise—I will return." He bowed his crowned head over my hand, then stood. He smiled a wicked smile and gave my hand a squeeze. "I *have* to return. I haven't tried your sandwiches yet."

There were so many things I wanted to say—questions, accusations, maybe even curse words—but the new Berron somehow scrambled my brain into a hum of crickets.

Maybe it was the magic.

Or maybe I liked him a little too much, in spite of myself.

Either way, he was gone through the Mirror before I could say a word. The multicolored magic shimmered, then subsided.

"Well, you've done it now," said Victorine. She scooped up Prospero's cane, spun it like a baton, and tucked it under her arm.

"You're one to talk." That red magic—it had been tampered with before I ever touched it. Only one of the Blessed could have done it. "You wanted this, didn't you? You were steering me all along. You just couldn't be seen to be doing it."

Victorine tilted her head, looked at me as if I were a monkey doing an especially clever circus trick. "How outlandishly false."

"What if I had done what he wanted me to? Locked the Seal forever? What would you have done then?"

Amusement played over her serene features. "If you are so full of curiosity, why have you not wondered about our compatriot?" She turned and walked toward the door.

"Oh, my God—*James*!" I holstered the knife and ran to catch up.

We found him sitting in the corridor. "About time you two showed up. It's been a regular St. Patrick's Day Parade out here."

I knelt next to him. "The crowds, the fighting, or the drinking?"

"The first two. The last one starts now, I hope." He used his shirt to dab at the cuts on his face.

I stood and offered my hand.

He took it and rose to his feet.

"What about the Mirror?" I said to Victorine. "Do we just leave it here? Now that it's open?"

"Do you suggest taking it to go?"

I pictured the three of us wrestling it past the model ships. "Probably not." Then I remembered Berron's smile—the sad one, not the wicked one. A handsome Prince. A dying land. Even the name sounded like poetry: The Fortress of Apples.

The other side of the Mirror was calling to me.

"Zelda?" said James. "Earth to Zelda. Come in, Zelda."

"Fine. It can stay. But I'm coming back," I said. "This isn't over."

Victorine smoothed a piece of hair away from my face, an odd gesture coming from her, laced with something like affection. "It is never over." She turned and led the way through the twisting corridors and back into the public area of the museum. Victorine paused, fished around in a pocket, and retrieved a roll of stickers. She peeled off three and stuck one on James's lapel, one on my tank top, and one on her own blouse. The white letters "NY" over "HS" emblazoned the dark orange-brown sticker.

"Now you are official," she said.

I poked at my sticker. "Do I get a discount at the gift shop?"

The final gallery was darker than the rest, the better to show off a large collection of lit Tiffany lamps. Dragonflies and daffodils, poppies and spiderwebs, glowed all around. In a way, they were a reflection of the paranormal world in all its messy glory: brilliantly colored, priceless, fragile, and—if knocked the wrong way—dangerously sharp.

A few steps more and we were outdoors, on the stairs facing busy Central Park West, and beyond it, the green trees of the park itself peeking over a stone wall.

Victorine stopped at the bottom of the steps. "James and I will return to Daniel. Where will you go now?"

The tree branches swayed in a sudden breeze. Even in the oppressive heat, the wind carried with it the promise of change. Time was passing. What was planted in the summer, ripened in the fall. I'd made an enemy. Saved a life. Kissed a Prince. Broken a Seal. All of those things would have their harvest.

Not to mention I still had a restaurant to finish.

But before I could take on the world, I needed to hold my true love in my arms. "I'm going home," I said. "To my little black poodle."

27

For the pre-opening party, I went with one of cousin Luella's easier recipes—a gluten-free rustic pie crust, the kind that's supposed to look freeform and messy. I tracked down the wild apple tree in Riverside Park and bagged as many of the little apples as I could find, then mixed the slices with plenty of sugar and cinnamon and hoped for the best. I didn't consider myself to be much of a pastry chef, so the fact that the wild apple galette came out of the oven unburned deserved to be chalked up as a total triumph.

I set it aside to cool and prepared toffee sauce to drizzle on for serving.

The caramel sugar scent combined with the smell of ham browning at James's station. He hummed a Nirvana song as the hot fat popped and sizzled.

"You really ought to update your playlist," I said.

"Oh, yeah?" He didn't take his eyes off the pan, carefully nudging the ham slices into even rows. "Well, the nineties called. They want your Doc Martens back."

I made a fist and thumped it into my chest as if I'd been stabbed. "Call an ambulance. I've been mortally wounded."

The bells on the door jangled. Georgiana and Jester dragged Poppy through the door like sled dogs without a sled. "It's the ham," she said, staggering inside. "I'm sure they'd be perfectly well-behaved otherwise."

I wiped my hands and came around the counter. Technically, dogs were only allowed on the outside patios of New York City restaurants, but this was my private party, so to hell with the rules. "Hello, boy!" I buried my fingers in Jester's thick head pouf and gave him his favorite scratches. He whipped his tongue at my hand in a determined and cheerful search for ham particles.

Poppy looked around. "Where shall we sit?"

"Anywhere you like."

Poppy slid into a seat next to one of the tables, and Georgiana sat on the floor next to her. Georgiana's tail swished back and forth over the tile, giving it one last polish before the rest of the guests arrived.

After one more pat for Jester, and a quick hand wash, I was back at it, assembling ingredients for the brunch sandwiches.

The bells barely had time to ring as my brother, Bruce, threw open the door. "I can't believe you actually did it." He strode inside, but stopped short when he saw Poppy. "Oh, hi, Poppy—didn't know you were going to be here." He ran his hand through his hair, then hurried to the bar stool farthest from the mind-reading fire witch.

"She's my roommate and my friend," I said. "And she's minding the dogs. Where did you think she was going to be?"

Bruce held up his hands. "Cool your jets. I just—you know—when there's a mind reader around, you want to have a minute to get your thoughts in order."

I raised an eyebrow. "What are *you* afraid of?"

Color rose in his cheeks.

He'd been avoiding her before, too. And now he'd turned into a blushing schoolboy? "Wait," I said. "Do you *like* her?"

The color turned brighter. "Just shut up, okay?"

"Okay, Romeo. Your secret's safe with me. I think. Unless I accidentally imagine you in a Cupid costume and she reads my mind."

"I'll kill you."

"You can try." I moved away to another kitchen section to chop vegetables for the Denver omelet sandwiches.

"Where's Daniel?" Bruce added.

"I'm not sure if he's coming. He hasn't been out much." It would have been more accurate to say *at all*. The recovery from conversion took time. I glanced up from the knife and bell pepper to catch Bruce's expression, which was somewhere between distaste and concern. Distaste at what Daniel had become, certainly, but probably even more to do with the fact that I'd been the one responsible. I sighed and swept the bell pepper pieces off the knife. You couldn't un-chop a vegetable, and you couldn't de-convert a vampire.

Meanwhile, James's humming had changed. I listened to a few bars, then threw a piece of green pepper at him. "No one said Soundgarden was an acceptable substitute."

He dodged, laughing.

Lily entered the shop with a cheerful "Hello!" and a wave. "It smells so good, Aunt Zelda!"

I smiled. "Got a station all fixed up for you so we can make you a sandwich and breakfast potatoes. And your mom's apple galette."

Lily slid onto a stool next to Bruce to watch the prep.

There's a rhythm to a working kitchen. Everything moves and rests at the right time. Your hands are reaching before you have to think of what's next. Cutting, pouring, stirring. Ingredients hit hot pans and sing a melody of cooking. Then you're gathering, assembling, bringing all the elements together until a harmonious plate appears like magic. It *is* magic. Especially when you set it in front of someone like an offering and they inhale with deep satisfaction.

The door rattled, but didn't open.

Lily sprang up. "I'll get that." She hurried to the glass door and held it open for Victorine—

And Daniel.

Who was walking with the help of Prospero's cane.

I'd walked through his door without a care in the world. Now he was walking through mine, a man I both knew and didn't know. What was he? *Who* was he? I stood rooted to the spot, unable to move as Victorine helped him sit.

He folded his hands over the grip of the cane and gazed at me. His eyes glowed red, of course, but that wasn't even what struck me. His eyes were the eyes of a man who has recalibrated his entire being. Despite the fact that he looked weak—that he had to be helped to walk—he radiated *power*.

My heart beat faster. And when I realized he could *tell* my heart was beating faster, it beat faster still.

I was a mess.

I caught myself staring, broke the gaze to wipe my hands on my apron and hurriedly grab a chilled carafe of fresh-squeezed orange juice and two glasses. I approached their table as if everything about this was completely ordinary. "Can I offer you a drink?"

"That's quite all right," said Victorine. She drew a silver flask and three tiny crystal goblets from her bag. How she carried them around without smashing them, I had no idea. "We brought our own." With that, she unscrewed the top of the flask and poured a thick red liquid into the goblets.

A *clang* sounded behind me.

James had let the pan slip. His head turned toward their table, and his nostrils flared. The red in his eyes burned brighter.

Victorine spoke. "Kindly tell James to join us."

I did as she asked.

James slid into an empty seat with barely concealed eagerness and accepted a glass.

Lily had swiveled around and was now watching. "What is that? Red wine?"

"Sagrantino," Victorine said smoothly. "It is an Italian variety. The name derives from the Latin for 'sacred.'"

"Can I try it?" said Lily.

"No!" I cleared my throat. "No, it's aged in casks sealed with wheat flour." I had no idea if that was true, but it *could* have been true.

Daniel raised his glass, caught my gaze again. "To Zelda."

"Oh, no, let's pick something else—"

"To Zelda," he said firmly.

"To Zelda," the other two echoed.

They drained their goblets. The "wine" stained their lips. Victorine's tongue darted out, catching a last drop. Daniel, on the other hand, let the red stain sit. He smiled at me.

I thought I might pass out.

"What's the matter, Zelda?" he asked. "Haven't you had breakfast yet?"

No, I was *not* going to be intimidated by my newly terrifying yet still sexy vampire ex-boyfriend. "Sure I have. Didn't you know? I eat *men* for breakfast." I flicked my kitchen towel at him and swung my hips as I walked back to the kitchen. "Come on, James," I called from my station. "We have a brunch to serve."

James dipped his head to Victorine, who nodded her regal permission to return to his duties.

We finished the prep in relative peace as my friends and relations gave themselves a tour of the place and made small talk. Before long,

I had the Denver omelet bagel sandwiches, breakfast potatoes, and ham plated and ready to serve. "All right, you miscreants, sit down."

Poppy and Lily were leaning on each other like old friends. "We're ladies who brunch!" said Poppy.

"Don't forget the dogs," said Bruce.

"Ladies, dogs, and gentlemen—enjoy." I dropped off plate after plate until everyone had one, including the dogs, who got their own plates of plain cooked egg. Then I took a seat for myself at the bar while James rejoined Victorine and Daniel. My own plate sat untouched on the bar behind me.

"Aren't you going to eat?" Bruce asked. Then he shoveled a forkful of breakfast potatoes into his mouth. "Man. These are as good as Grandma's."

"Is that a compliment I hear?"

"Don't let it go to your head." He went back to devouring his Denver omelet bagel sandwich.

I picked up my own sandwich and took a bite. Fluffy eggs; hot but still crisp green bell pepper pieces; warm, melted sharp cheddar; toasted and buttered bagel.

I finally rose to slice the wild apple galette. I plated the slices and drizzled each one with toffee sauce, then delivered them while James fiddled with the radio in search of good music. Forks clinked on plates in a syncopated rhythm with eighties pop.

When the apple galette was nothing but crumbs, Poppy dragged my brother off his stool and began to dance to the music. Lily carried Jester like he was a little black lamb and gently rocked him to the beat. Georgiana put her paws on James's shoulders and shuffled back and forth with him. I floated through, adding my own dance moves to each pair before moving on.

Victorine and Daniel watched it all.

I moved to the window. The morning sunlight cast shadows from the old-school gold-lettered font spelling out "West Side Sandwiches." While I stood there, I heard a strange sound that came from outside: a fast *clip-clop*, *clip-clop* that rattled against the synthesizer sounds coming from the radio.

I glanced behind me. No one else had heard it yet.

Then I saw the horse.

It was dappled gray, but so dark that the splashes of white looked like stars and galaxies in the night sky. No saddle. And on the horse's back, a man with such easy grace he made riding a horse down the street look like the most natural thing someone could do. Beams of sunlight flashed on his golden crown, and tiny gold sparks struck under the horse's hooves. He stopped in front of the restaurant and swung down like a dancer.

I slipped outside.

"I have come to claim my sandwich," Berron said, with an impish twinkle in his eyes.

"You're riding a horse."

"Yes."

"In Manhattan."

"So it seems." He peered over my shoulder, through the window.

"Aren't you a little concerned, parading about in broad daylight like this? On a *horse*?"

Berron turned his attention back to me with an expression of mild surprise. "Of course not. We'll all return soon. But I won't bring you any more unwanted attention now, if it bothers you. I'll even go without brunch." He paused, then swooped in for a kiss on my cheek before I could blink. "Don't worry. I'll come back for you soon."

"Come back for me? What does that mean?"

Berron smiled, then turned and re-mounted his horse. A breeze spun down the street with the scent of turning leaves. "Goodbye, my Zelda." He clicked his tongue and the horse launched into a trot. He turned and called back, his baritone voice fading as they raced in the direction of Central Park, "You still owe me a sandwich!"

"I'm not your Zelda!" I called back.

The door opened, and a different male voice rumbled behind me. "Showoff," Daniel said. He was leaning on Prospero's cane. "I could ride a horse if I wanted to."

"He said he's coming back for me."

"He also called you 'his' Zelda."

"Well, I'm not," I huffed.

"Hmm." Daniel limped closer. "Good to know."

"He didn't even get a sandwich."

Daniel raised his eyebrows. "He did get a kiss."

"This is not some kind of weird sandwich-and-kisses trading post." I rolled my eyes, blew out a breath. "Fine. I can't have my first customer review be a one-star, so, here—" I kissed his cheek only as long as necessary to inhale his cologne and feel his stubble sting my lips. Okay, maybe it was a couple of seconds longer. "Happy now?"

"Very."

I held out my arm. "Shall we?" He took my arm. Vampire magic curled between us as we walked back inside.

Every place has its boundaries: the threshold of a doorway; the iron fence around a private park; the water that rings Manhattan. Boundaries between normal and weird. Friend and foe. Right and wrong. This mundane world, and somewhere else entirely.

I'd crossed more than a few boundaries already. But I had to believe Grandma would have been proud. That if she had been there, she would have clapped me on the shoulder, smiled, and said "That's my granddaughter." She, more than anyone else, would have understood what I had done. We were connected by family, by time, by blood and magic, by existing in a universe that didn't always stay tame and predictable and easy.

We were strong. We had to be. And if I had done wrong, I would put it right. If I fell, I'd stand up and keep going. I had a restaurant to run and a city that was mine as much as it had been hers. If I didn't fit in, I'd just have to be the freeform, gluten-free pie crust that tastes better than a perfectly round conventional one. I'd be the peppers on the ham, egg, and cheese bagel.

As soon as Jester saw me come in, he wiggled wildly in Lily's arms.

I hurried to her and scooped him up, burying my face in his puppy-scented fluff. Handsome princes and powerful vampires were all well and good, but what really mattered was holding my little black poodle, in my restaurant, in the greatest city in the world.

Our New York story had begun, and it was going to be deliciously magical.

ALSO BY KATE MOSEMAN

Masks and Mirrors
Flames and Frying Pans
Witch and Wolfhound

Silver Spells
Silver Charms
Silver Dreams
Silver Shadows

A Good Demon Is Hard to Find
A Witch's Work Is Never Done
An Angel in My Teacup

Roller Coaster Romance